END OF TERM

END OF TERM

ALASTAIR DUNNETT

A CRIME CLUB BOOK
DOUBLEDAY
NEW YORK LONDON TORONTO SYDNEY AUCKLAND

A Crime Club Book
Published by Doubleday, a division of
Bantam Doubleday Dell Publishing Group, Inc.
666 Fifth Avenue, New York, New York 10103

Doubleday and the portrayal of a man
with a gun are trademarks of
Doubleday, a division of Bantam Doubleday Dell
Publishing Group, Inc.

Library of Congress Cataloging-in-Publication Data

Dunnett, Alastair MacTavish, 1908–
End of term / Alastair Dunnett.
p.   cm.
"A Crime Club book."
I. Title.
PR6054.U557E5   1989
823'.914—dc19   89-31313
CIP

ISBN 0-385-24673-0
October 1989
First Edition
OG

For Ninian

END OF TERM

1

Barry Raeburn whistled the practice game to a stop and waved the players up to him. He had driven them hard, but they had enjoyed it, wanting more. They ran to him from the scattered parts of the field, forming a semicircle to await his commendation or rebuke. There were thirty of them, hardly any of them above seventeen years old and almost none of them daring to think he might be touched by the fame that had come to Raeburn in his teens. Yet it pleased them to receive his mild strictures and to show that they understood him. At forty-three, he had reached an age beyond their comprehension.

But they could at least emulate his maturity. So it suited them to fall into postures. As his eye fell round the group, he could see the ones who tried to conceal their exhausted breathing, as if they had not run themselves to the end of their tether for the past eighty minutes. These, when they came to manhood, would be the poseurs, forever putting a better face on their talents and performance, and some of them all through life would get away with it. Others, less careful of appearances, puffed and blew hugely, guessing that an appearence of honesty might serve them better than any affectation. Most of the others took up attitudes that they had seen struck by admired athletes at halftime: the arms clasped behind the head, the bent back with hands on knees, the jumping, the shoulder-swinging, the doubled-up crouching. Raeburn loved them for it, all that endless willingness to learn from their elders, like fox cubs and young otters.

"Okay, chaps—that's not bad. Mr. Rankine will take you for a few special exercises. You've ten or fifteen minutes more of decent light." Ian Rankine, one of the teachers, had trotted over to them from the touchline. Raeburn tossed the whistle to him and made briskly for the touchline. Their laughter followed him, and the sound of the whistle calling them to task.

It took Raeburn only seconds to reach the touchline, where a knot of four or five girls were gathered. They were huddled in a giggling circle, all speaking at once. In the short time it took him to reach them, there had flashed through his mind some of the appalling minor essentials on which he had had to judge scarcely two terms ago, when it had been decided they should take in a small quota of girls. It was understood that in educational terms they would be exceptional and frighteningly mature, compared with the lumbering, well-meaning lads who had been the school's population until then. It had something to do with moving with the times, he understood.

Of all the inevitable embarrassments, the greatest discomfiture for him had come from the visit of the official school uniform adviser, who had arrived with samples and swatches of material, and who had him summed up at once, upon her arrival, as a bachelor and thereby deficient.

They had agreed on the blazer, a drab maroon with brass buttons. "Now, the skirts," she proceeded briskly. "Serge. Nothing beats serge. Of course it gets shiny, but that keeps down the pride of the girls whose people overdress them at home. . . ."

He ventured, "I understand there are ways you can reduce the shine on serge." Understand? He knew. He had had to do it.

"I think you are talking about men's suits, not young ladies' skirts." The implacable bullying went on. "You have a lot to learn, headmaster."

She went on. "Then we have to think of what you might call the underpinnings. I take it you are not thinking of stockings and suspender belts."

"Not in this context," he found himself conceding.

"Good! As to other items . . ." She had ground on, showing no mercy.

"We can safely leave that to the mothers, or whoever guides them at home."

"I don't agree. But we'll come back to that later. I hope you will agree that shoes and sports gear should be entirely uniform. Personal choice allowed in trainers and such. Are you in the picture?"

"I believe so. Your organization informed me that you would come here to assist and advise me, but there was no word about admonishment."

"But—"

"The next step will be for you to take your samples away, and to have them and others sent to me along with appropriate recommendations. I shall obtain expert advice on them . . . Mrs. Gibson, the matron, will give you tea before you go. Or perhaps you would prefer something stronger?" He could not remember that she had said anything more.

By this time he had joined the girls, who had turned their backs on the playing pitch and were heading for the school buildings. He felt the wind chill on the patches of his face that were flushed from the memory of his encounter with the clothes woman.

"Going my way?" he asked. It was the kind of banality they were entitled to expect. They were still getting to know him.

"Yes," they chorused. At least one added, "Sir."

"I thought you might have waited to see the end of the practice," he said as they walked. "You know—encouraging the gladiators."

They gave him a laugh with mock scorn in it, and he knew which one would make the reply.

And in she came with, "There's a man-child or two out there who have had enough encouragement for one day." He joined them in their knowing laughter. She was Elaine Grandison, the star of the small flock, already aware of her potential but holding it in check until she might find a more promising arena. She was to go next year to some finishing school in Switzerland, and he imagined that by the age of twenty-two she would be married to some European aristocrat with expectations, which would not, of course, be higher than hers. Or she might be a nun, or an interior decorator, or hanging about hoping to get into films. If only he could be certain that here at Markland, for this short time, they were giving her all they could.

Frances Allen said, "We thought we should encourage ourselves with coffee before prep . . ."

"I hear you are coping," he told them.

"One thing I've always wanted to ask you, headmaster," said Frances. "Was it actually twenty-seven rugby caps you got for Scotland?"

"About that. It's kind of an old story."

"Where do you keep them all?"

"In a drawer somewhere, all wrapped in tissue paper."

"What I wanted to know, sir," Frances said, "would you lend us five or six for a sketch we are doing for the school revue next term? We'll be careful not to damage them."

"Of course. Let me know nearer the time. We'd better get this term finished first."

He left them at the drive to their house and ran the rest of the way round the main building to the back entrance to his rooms. If he had been a married headmaster, there would have been a house for him, apart, on the grounds. But he had settled for a suite on the ground floor at the rear, where he could watch the sports fields.

He met the matron in the back hall. "Shower and tea, Mrs. Gibson," he said. "Anything doing?"

"Nothing to worry about. Are you remembering you are to have a late night?"

"Only too well. I'll lie down later for an hour or two. Thanks."

After the shower, the changing, and the gulped tea, he found

Mrs. Gibson hovering again. "Before you go in, Mr. Raeburn—headmaster—I've just shown Lord Melfort into your lounge. He's staying at Kintalla Castle and wants to see you urgently. I told him to help himself to a drink."

He gave her a nod. "No doubt he'll waste no time."

She went on. "Will you see young Michael Mackay first? He's waiting in the front hall."

"Mackay? He should be in bed by now."

He found himself saying the same thing to the fifteen-year-old who greeted him and was now answering, "Just a final check, sir. Can I meet you here at one-thirty A.M.? And the visitor—is he coming?"

"Yes—driving late from near Dumfries. Bed for you at once."

"Right away, sir. Conditions look good tonight."

When he got at last to his room, he found Lord Melfort already installed there, in the best armchair.

"Come in," Lord Melfort said, waving a glass of brandy towards his host, with a welcoming flourish. "Make yourself at home. You can see that I have done so. Not a bad brandy, I may say. Does this come off headmaster's wages?"

"We manage," Raeburn told him. "It is generally here for visitors only, especially the resourceful ones who can find it for themselves. I never touch the stuff myself." He opened his cupboard where the few bottles were stacked. "My tastes lie nearer home. If you don't mind . . ." He helped himself to a small dram and took a seat. "Your health! What brings you to these parts?" They drank, warily, old and suspicious acquaintances.

Melfort said, "There wouldn't perhaps be a decent cigar in the place?"

"Second drawer in the cabinet on your left. Cutter, lighter, ashtray."

Melfort was already rummaging. In a moment he was dipping, squeezing, smelling, lighting. "A present, I suppose, from the Duke, your patron? You do yourself well here, Raeburn—if on a somewhat small scale. Allow me to get this cigar going." He devoted himself to the task.

Raeburn watched him. This man had been an early actor on the stage of the Foreign Office, gaining eventually and soon the two best British embassies where, as a contemporary remarked, he had made ambassadorship look easy. Now retired and vigorous, he had contrived to have himself appointed to the main boards of one of the most aggressive British multinational companies. Although Raeburn did not know this, he had succeeded in blackmailing the man who had built it up, a certain Duke of long lineage who was undoubtedly the most celebrated businessman of that eminence.

"Yes," said Melfort. "I am staying at Kintalla Castle. Ostensibly I am here for some fishing and shooting, but I have other affairs on hand. The Duchess has made me very comfortable. As you would expect. The Duke, you may not know, has become almost permanently resident in France. We have large business interests there, but you can take it from me he has some political business afoot." Melfort paid attention to the cigar.

Raeburn, waiting, felt the familiar surge of dislike that had been his main feeling the few times he had encountered this man. There was some basic dishonesty there. Already Raeburn seethed within at the man's offhand reference to the Duchess. She was the younger sister of a rugby-playing mate of his. He had known her from her girlhood, and he had been astonished to find her here as the Duke's wife. They had shared a perilous adventure, in which Melfort had also played a part (but not nobly).

"Are you to stay at Kintalla for some time?" Raeburn asked.

"Not long. The ostensible reason is that I may enjoy some of the sporting facilities of the estate, but the main purpose is more important. We arrived only yesterday afternoon."

"We?" Raeburn asked, anxious to clear the ground before the making of some demand whose onset he was feeling in the air. "You always seemed to me to be someone who travelled alone."

"You are, as ever, most perceptive." The man studied Raeburn with what, in one less adroit, would have been insolence. "However, if you come to know me better, you will become aware that I have never been able to make it a habit, as you apparently have, to evade the good things that make life comfortable. I have a companion with me, a complaisant female creature. The Duchess was most understanding when I announced that I was intending to arrive *à deux*. She arranged indeed that even our meals will be served in our suite. I mentioned, of course, that the Duke had agreed."

Raeburn said, "You and the Duke have much in common." He found it hard to keep the hatred from showing in his eyes.

"You are right. Although I think I should prefer not to notice a slight emphasis on the word 'common.'" Melfort by this time was well into his cigar. "However, I am here to talk serious business with you."

"Please go on."

"You will remember, Raeburn—that the last time we came together was over a matter of constitutional moment that seemed to be concerned with the well-being of this country."

"Of course I remember. At that time I believed I was suffering from a fatal disease, and the Duke contrived that I be brought to this school as a teacher. He had assembled a group, of which you were one, which believed that there was a plot to kidnap a royal prince who was a pupil here. But it turned out that the kidnap attempt was made on the Duke's own infant son. This happened, and we were able to foil it, violently. Enough?"

"More or less. You may remember that I myself played a sizeable part in the action," Melfort said. "But I am now on a different tack. I do not believe that, simply because the Duke is not now resident, others may not turn our minds to important projects. Before I go into details, would you care to confirm that this school is about to set up a well-equipped junior institute of technology?"

"That is right. We have received a very handsome anonymous donation to make this possible."

Melfort gave him a knowing nod. "Anonymous, of course. But the donation came from the Duke himself. Correct?"

"It is, of course, from the Duke's fortune, but the expenditure is at the discretion of the Duchess and has much to do with her decision to remain at Kintalla."

"Quite. The fact remains, Raeburn, that the Duke, for reasons best known to himself, has been most generous to you."

"Melfort, I have never denied it." To hell with this fellow. What was he up to?

There had slipped across the other man's face a diplomatic coldness that had brought the quakes to many an underling. "Would you care also to confirm that you have as a pupil in this school a young fellow of exceptional electronic talent—a skill with gadgets and such—which could be said to be unique?"

"Right. 'Genius' is probably the word. Michael Mackay by name. What has he got to do with this—with you?"

"As you are about to learn, this is the whole point. I take it that we are talking in confidence?"

Raeburn simply stared at him, and Melfort went on coolly. "Some friends and I have a mind to be the custodians of certain scientific developments, and we are looking for a safe centre where they can be developed. Scientific progress has immediate values, and with your cooperation they could be profitable . . . for all concerned. You would appear to fit into the scheme. What about it? In fact, at this time, since I have given you some valuable information, there is very little choice left. Are you in?"

"How do you know about this pupil? There has been no publicity."

"Publicity is a coarse word. I have never dealt in publicity. But let me say—interesting facts have a habit of getting out, especially in the direction of those who can make good use of them. There will be no danger of leakage from our side. I think you had better make up your mind to come in; then you will be put fully in the picture."

Raeburn stood up. "I am insulted that you do not know anything of me, Melfort, although yours is not the kind of acquaintance I have ever sought. Neither I nor my school will have anything to do with what you seem to be proposing. It's on a par with some of your other schemes."

Melfort was on his feet. "You speak dangerously, Raeburn."

"I mean to. It's clear that, whatever you have in mind, it is certainly beyond the law. You can take the whole scheme and yourself away from here."

The years of indulgence that Melfort had enjoyed were now at last showing in the gathering of flesh below his chin, from which the flush of his anger was mounting to his brow, where the hair was receding. He almost trembled with the effort of controlling his instincts—to appear and sound reasonable. As he spoke, it was through another layer of distaste that he had to deal with this inferior who dared to turn aside this chance of sudden gain.

"But dammit, man—you know enough about me to be well aware that I generally get what I want. There's nothing more to this chance than the role you took on in the kidnap plot. You were the man inside then. And that was far enough beyond the law."

"That time we set out to outwit a wee scheme got up by a gang of criminals, and we were on the side of the law and of justice. Let me make it clear. I believe you have it in mind to profit by robbing the public interest in some way which, thank God, you haven't yet described. But you have said enough. Even if I were as corrupt as you hoped, you could not hide your plan. One of your thieves would talk. And not only this school but every other such place in the country would never be credible again. No, I tell you. You will never be able to guess what an affront your proposal is. Out!"

"God, Raeburn, this could finish you!" Melfort said. He ground out the half-smoked cigar in the silver receptacle that stood on the small table. It was a large engraved quaich which a New Zealand Caledonian club had presented to Raeburn after a successful season as captain of a touring team.

He took the quaich gently in his hands and tipped the contents into the open fire. He flicked the folded silk handkerchief from Melfort's breast pocket, carefully wiped the inside, and laid it down again. Then he stuffed the handkerchief back into the pocket.

"Time to go," he said. "Show yourself out, and don't come back."

Melfort turned and went to the door like a volcano, slamming it behind him. Again he was thwarted, for the compressed air cylinder that controlled it hissed behind him, easing the door gently closed. Raeburn could hear his footsteps down the corridor. He went smiling towards a drawer where there was a chamois cloth, and he rubbed the silver lovingly with it.

There was a tap on the door, and before he had time to imagine that Melfort had come back, it opened, and a bright pair of eyes looked through.

"In or out?" said the voice with the eyes, and Roy Baillie stepped into the room.

"In. Glad to see you, Roy," he said, for he had been expecting him.

Baillie said, "So who was the breenging fellow with the red face who passed me on the way out? He didn't seem all that pleased about your hospitality. I thought I recognized him. . . . Somebody I know?"

"Surprised you remember him, although he was a debonair chap when you met him the first time. It was when you were captain of a Scottish XV touring France—it wasn't yesterday—and I was with you as a junior with my first representative honour. He was the British Ambassador in Paris, and he gave us a reception—of sorts."

"By God, yes! With some reluctance, as I remember. He seemed to suggest that he had been conned into it by the First

Secretary, good old Jimmy Melvin, and that we were not quite up to scratch socially. What's he up to now, and why the naughty temper?"

"You could say he had fallen on evil days. In fact, it seems to me he is the one who makes the days evil. But forget him. Let's get you settled and then talk about what brings you here."

At supper later, with drams going, they sat at the fireside.

Baillie was saying, "When you told me about this whiz kid you had, I got the Trust to cough up five hundred pounds for him to buy some apparatus. I agreed with you that I should come down and have a look at our investment. So here I am, and I may say I'm pretty glad to see you in such good nick. You had a lot of us worried."

"So I got away with it. But no more of that. You'll like Michael Mackay. Good young chap—still fifteen—it seems we can't teach him here any more about maths and technology. I really haven't much of a clue about what he is up to. We gave him the top storey of the old tower in the original building. Littered with junk."

"I can hardly wait. What we do in the Trust is to back individual talent, and there isn't so much of it around." They spoke on for a time. Baillie was already a senior QC and should be on the bench in a year or two.

Raeburn said, "I suppose it all came out about this time last year. I had made tentative steps towards setting up a technology department to give a scientific grounding to pupils bent in that direction. Mackay turned up in these first classes, and they saw he was totally absorbed in the whole range of what goes on in the world. Seems he had been mopping it up somehow since he was in the primary. Beyond anything the boffin I brought in to get the thing going had ever seen. So we simply let him set up his own show. I don't suppose you'll understand much of it anymore than I do, but at least you'll see it."

"One-thirty in the hall, I think you said."

Raeburn rose. "Yes. We'd better turn in. It looks like being a long night."

2

They were up and about by 1 A.M. Raeburn made them a hot drink, and they walked about the big kitchen, mugs in hand, talking.

Baillie was saying, "It's terrific to see you here, Barry. Markland has always had the best reputation for the production of independent chaps and some quite scholarly thinkers. I had heard, though, that the man who started it all was getting to be on the old side. They must have been glad to get you."

"I was lucky. I happened to be there at the right time. It has its rewards—especially when the occasional really bright one turns up."

"Now it seems you have an electronic genius on your hands."

"Yes, I believe he is. Genius is a word I don't much use, but it is true in this case."

"Barry, I've heard the word genius applied to you many a time, for your displays on the international rugby field." Raeburn grimaced mildly. "You may also be a genius as a teacher and headmaster, for all I know."

"Did I thank you for getting the money?"

"You did. And the young fellow wrote me as well."

"Good for him. Tell me something about that charity you run."

"I don't run it. We have a director, and some of us advise as trustees. It's a small organization. We try to find funds for the backing of what might turn out to be exceptional talent; it might be in music or the arts, in sports or in some other area, as long as there's potential."

"It sounds like a great idea. You really must see this lad for yourself. He spent most of your money on gadgets like aerials and dishes and bits of junk that he picked up here and there. I haven't a clue what he does, and he isn't all that keen to show me, but I've made sure he'll show you. He can actually pick up by radar, or something, the movement of ships in the Atlantic. He has shown me that much anyway. I felt I had to report some of this to the authorities. An Admiralty chap phoned me. He obviously didn't believe a word of what I told him, and he lost me in a welter of questions full of jargon. He wants to come and see for himself. I thought you had better get in first."

"There is nobody here who can teach Mackay anything, and the people at Cambridge say they want him for some course as soon as he can come, young as he is. When I told him that, he said he would like to think about it. The reason being that he didn't want to be wasting his time on theory. That's the kind of kid he is."

Michael Mackay was waiting for them in the hall. He shook hands readily with Baillie. "Thank you, sir, for the money you were good enough to send me. It's been very useful."

"That's what money's for. Is it all spent?"

"Pretty nearly. I'll show you."

Raeburn said, "Suppose you go on ahead and open up your place, Michael. We'll follow." The lad turned and ran.

"He looks nothing like a swot," Baillie was musing as they walked. "I would have said he was something like a good man in the junior cross-country, and probably important in the junior rugby team. No thick glasses, no adenoids—only the least sign of acne."

"Ordinary, in fact. As he is a kind of special case, I have lately been allowing him to sleep in the afternoon so that he can sometimes work all night in his lab. I installed him in that ancient tower in the south building. Tangles of wire and flashing lights. The only time I had half an hour there with him, he showed me on a screen what he said was a Russian submarine in the North

Sea. I sent a letter to the Ministry of Defence, but I don't think they took it seriously, although they are sending that expert from the Admiralty next week."

They climbed the dusty stairs of the tower and went through the open door of the room at the top. It was a drab place, dimly lit, with the boy politely standing up for them in a welter of wires and humming instruments.

"I hope there's something special," Raeburn said.

"There is always something special." Mackay pushed a chair forward for Baillie and lifted over a box for the headmaster. They settled down.

Baillie said, "You might as well know that I'm just an ignorant lawyer. I don't understand a thing about all this gadgetry."

"Nobody does," the boy said tolerantly. "Well, almost nobody. Don't worry—I'll explain it as simply as I can. After all, it's your money—a lot of it."

"You took the words right out of my mouth," Baillie said. It made for the first laugh.

The men stood for a moment, looking round the square room. Night had made the windows dark, but they could tell that they had a wide view of the coast and the sea down towards Ireland, and away to the north. Young Mackay closed the curtains and then made a gesture at the shelves packed with ticking and moaning boxes and moving dials. He said, "We'll not bother describing all this stuff just now. Do you mind if we concentrate on the screen?"

He switched on clicking knobs at a side panel and said, "We'll have to wait a bit. Takes a while to warm up."

"What is this, anyway?" Baillie asked.

"This is my viewing screen. Interesting things there at this time of night."

"It looks," Baillie said, "kind of homemade. Is it expensive?"

"No. I made it myself. . . . In fact—oh, excuse me a minute." The boy took a pair of headphones from a shelf and held them towards the headmaster. "Sir, do you mind putting these on for a moment? There might be something interesting coming through." Without waiting for a reply, he clamped them over Raeburn's ears and turned to Baillie.

"You see, Mr. Raeburn can't hear a thing now. I didn't want to tell him this story. Don't you tell him, will you sir? In fact, the screen is a replacement glass for a lavatory door that someone broke. I intercepted it when it was delivered for the joiner, and I expect that another one has been ordered. Anyway, I needed it badly. The image is coming up . . . a minute. I'll release the head." He turned to lift the earphones off Raeburn with, "We'll not bother about sound signals at the moment, sir. Come and see the screen."

They bent over, and the screen started to flicker. Baillie asked, "Have you ever seen a camera obscura?"

"No," Mackay said eagerly. "Have you? This is the same principle. The trouble with all these electronic chaps is that they try to do everything solely by electronics. A lot of very clever people have worked on other principles for hundreds of years, and they made marvellous discoveries. Everything should be used. Wait a minute—it won't be long now. . . ." He was working two calibrated slides, one with each hand, that ran along the top and the sides of the screen, and his concentration was fierce, but he took time to say, "These are latitude and longitude—I am after something special—not long now. . . ."

The screen was now apparently fully lit, pale green and tumultuous, with what looked like wave patterns. There was a blob of light near the middle, and Mackay focussed so that it sharpened into a shape. They stared at this.

"Recognize it?" he asked. "It's Rockall. You have to reverse the colours. The shape stays the same."

They got it then. It was Rockall, the bleak sea-battered cone of rock far out from their shores in the Atlantic, that had been the centre of some diplomacy on the question of who owned it, and how far it could be reckoned an outcrop of mainland territory, and especially who might be the imperial owner of the wealth of oil deposit believed to lie in the depths round its base. They had to stretch their imagination, for what they saw, instead of the black peak, was a pale outline surrounded by a creamy sea, and the huge white waves beating and climbing on it were black and full of movement. The sea was empty.

"That's amazing! How far are we from the scene?" Baillie asked.

"Oh, about four hundred miles, roughly. From this point I can get clear to it, avoiding the Mull of Kintyre and the point of Islay."

By this time they were as intent as he was. "Tell us something about how this is done."

Mackay nodded. "All right. But I may have to stop halfway through. There's a Russian submarine out there, and I want to see what he does. He's been there for a few days—generally out of sight from here, on the other side of the island. We might be busy tonight."

He spoke for about ten minutes while the three of them pored over the lit screen. It was all ridiculously beyond Raeburn and Baillie, but later they wrote down some of the phrases. Suddenly he waved them aside, focussing again, and saying, "Here's the Russian."

He had brought the picture up to about twice its original size. From the rear of the Rock there slid a white shape, fully surfaced, a long pale pencil with the unmistakable lines of a conning tower.

"No hiding, you see. They all know what the other chap is doing. We'll have more visitors. . . ." The shape was now clearly in view, but distant. He traced the outline with a finger. "It's one of their Delta-class subs—from the Northern fleet. They come through the Iceland gap, and they are always around at this time of night. There must be a regular Rockall patrol. Lots of ballistic missiles aboard that fellow. . . . Let's have a look north."

The picture slid away, and new vastness of sea came up. With another blob, and then another.

"That one there—that is *Odinn,* the Iceland patrol ship. He has to bounce about here at most times of the year, I suppose, to make the point that they think Rockall is theirs. One gun—you can see it—and a helicopter below deck.

"That's an Irish patrol ship. I think this is the first time they have been here. Not their biggest—small armament."

He moved the picture again, scanning to the south. "Yes—there's the Scottish Fishery Protection vessel—one of them—*Vigilant,* I think. He'll go away when his big brother turns up." He was scanning with his nose six inches from the screen. "Here they are! Two County-class destroyers, in company."

The two slugs moved into the picture from the bottom, and, as they watched, parted as they neared Rockall to circumnavigate, each from a different side. The British ships emerged on opposite sides and joined up. For a moment the one on the western course seemed to shave the submarine, merging into the other shape.

"I suppose you know who's missing?" Mackay asked matter-of-factly.

"Denmark," Baillie tried. "They always seem to be claiming territorial rights to Rockall."

"Yes, but they almost never show up. I was looking for the Americans. They want to be in on every show."

"Tell me—how do you get these pictures from all that distance?"

"The elevation beam, to match the surface one, is coming from a satellite up there. I'd better not tell you which satellite, but I am tapping it."

"I suppose that's illegal," Baillie suggested.

"I suppose it is," Mackay said. And they got back to the screen.

"Here they come," he said, pointing to a small group worming in from the bottom left of the screen. "It's the Americans."

"A cruiser—a big fellow—yes, one of the Truxton class. And two destroyers—the Americans always overdo it. I haven't found out yet what they do, but they seem to pick up all sorts of signals —maybe mine. That would be funny."

The little bright toy outlines moved up the screen, and there seemed to be a convergence as the other milky shadows flickered toward the Rock, all of them ringing it like a cricket outfield.

"Now there's something that usually turns up." They looked at the squat shape coming in from the top corner. "Russian. It's a Balzan-class intelligence collector ship, the sort that is always following the Americans and us round the Atlantic."

After a time the whole formation of the big power ships was in a circle, navigating round Rockall. It was silent in the tower, but they could imagine the clamour of the wind and the sea, and the beat of huge engines, and the crackle of signals.

Baillie saw a speck of light break away from one of the smaller ships and drift towards the island. "What's that?" he asked, pointing.

Mackay was on the alert at once. He fumbled below his table and seemed to turn some knob. The picture almost doubled in size again, bringing them up to Rockall.

"Where did it come from?"

"That ship," Baillie told him.

"The Irishman. Let's have a look." The picture almost doubled in size again, cutting out the circling ships. "It's his helicopter. It looks as if he is trying a landing."

As it hovered over the summit of the Rock, the larger ships were encroaching towards the centre.

"They have searchlights on the chopper—all of them. Trying to blind the pilot, I guess." He turned to switch on a radio set on a side table. "It's a German radio I picked up cheap. I have it permanently turned to the international navigation wavelength. They all use it in the clear for quick surface communication. They're probably talking now."

The set came on with a click and a whine, and at once there

was a voice, speaking the precise English of a Russian who has been taught by an American. ". . . time to go home. No Irish games here." And then, "No trespassing." The two small ships eased gradually out of sight, and Mackay brought the picture back to its original size.

He said, "It's a good show, isn't it? Very clear tonight. You're lucky."

"Do they ever shoot?" Raeburn asked. A daft question, as he well knew, but he couldn't think of any other.

"I don't think so. I'm not sure I could get anything like that on the screen. Well, unless one of them got sunk, and he would disappear, of course. I think I once saw a Russian firing a missile, but there was nobody else about. A dummy, I expect—they would pick it up at sea for tests. Look! They're on fast speeds now, trying each other out."

The shapes had not formed their circle again, but went darting and pushing into each other's groupings. They were still at their games, but practising undoubtedly for the time when the games might be real. They were already drawing away and the screen was emptying, with Mackay announcing that he could not hold on to his satellite any longer. Sure enough, the screen flickered to emptiness. He switched it off.

Later, when it was already first light, he showed them out politely. Baillie had a final question. "Will you be giving a demonstration of all this to the man from the Admiralty? Or the Cambridge people?"

"I don't think so. They would just complicate the interrelated assemblies, and it would take them years, working on the principles they use. Anyway, I'm meaning to junk most of this stuff, although I'll probably come back to it later. There's something else I want to build, and I must get it finished by Christmas at the latest."

"That sounds exciting. What next, then?" Baillie asked.

Mackay said, "I think another supernova is going to turn up shortly, and I want to be ready for it."

Raeburn and his guest walked slowly in the dawn towards the main building. After a silence Raeburn said, "A black mark to the man who first speaks of babes and sucklings."

"Agreed." His guest nodded. "I'll have to think about it all. I don't know what to make of it. But he's worth backing, that's for sure." He laughed, and stretched in the morning air. "I suppose that science lends itself to some astonishingly naive breakthroughs."

"We don't know enough about it yet. I doubt you could get these conditions in your field of law."

"You couldn't. We're too embedded in our procedures. . . . I think I'll take to the road right away, Barry. If I go now, I can get on top of a horrid brief by midday. Thanks for letting me in on the first Battle of Rockall."

In the hours before his secretary arrived, Raeburn sat in his office and dictated some letters and memoranda. There were innumerable requests from parents who would come for the end-of-term day in a few days' time, and who wanted to talk with him about younger brothers and sisters of some present pupil, or whether their son should think of Sandhurst, or the father's engineering business, or nursing, or the stage. A formidable Lord Lieutenant wanted to enquire if he might have the privilege of proposing the vote of thanks to Raeburn and his staff at the closing ceremony; there were applications; questions about how far private tuition might be available in Greek, or Turkish, or Russian, or karate; what was the level of singing instruction; could the girl bring her pony and learn to ride sidesaddle; they were atheists and did not want their son exposed to such ordeals as morning prayers; a television company wanted a crew to spend most of a term following the progress of, say, three particular pupils, and could they be guaranteed that the product would not be censored before transmission?

He worked his way through the replies and handed the tapes to his secretary, Jo Anne Stevenson, in time to join the junior morning run, twice round the grounds. Afterwards he sat in with the careers master and five seniors, leaving this term, and talked about where they should go and what they should do. Few of them believed him when he told them that he himself had had the same doubts and apprehensions at the same age.

This gave him time to marshall a group of seniors, load them into the school's minibus, and drive them to the moors, where they climbed some modest tops, racing to cairns and gathering there, knowing that it was the last time that they would all be together. They ate sandwiches, and on the way down (he had planned this) they came to a remote waterfall and a deep cold pool. Here he made them strip and plunge, joining in their cries of freedom and mock agony as they felt the sting of the intense cold built up by the months the waters had lain in high snow beds.

At last they drove back to the school grounds, and he dispersed them to their tasks. Jo Anne Stevenson hurried across the paving to where he had parked the car.

"I've been waiting for you, headmaster. Panic stations."

"What's the problem?"

"Bad news. I haven't told anyone else. There was a call from Kintalla Castle. Lord Melfort has been found shot dead on the moor. Apparently by accident. They found him about eleven this morning. The police have been there. Apparently no foul play suspected. The Duchess would like you to phone her."

"Of course." They trotted to the main building and his office. When he heard her voice, his first words were, "Edith, tell me."

"Not much to tell. Reid and Macfarlane, the two gamekeepers, found him. They had heard a shot and guessed he was too near to raise any hares or birds. It was the old story. He had been climbing a fence without breaking his gun. It must have fouled wire or clothing, and he took the discharge in his stomach. Death was instantaneous. They brought him back on a gate."

"Where is he?"

"I got on to his lawyer in London, and he took over. The undertakers arrived a few minutes ago from Ayr, and they took him away. . . . Barry, I wouldn't mind seeing you, if you can make it."

"I'll come to you now," he said.

3

He had time, or so he fancied, to get to his rooms and change from the hill boots into dry shoes. But as he rushed back through the hall, there was a firm hand on his shoulder and a voice that said to him with authority, "No you don't!"

Mrs. Gibson, the school's matron, was there with an admonitory finger in his face.

"Jo Anne has put me in the picture. You are not leaving here in that condition. I have started a hot bath for you. Get in there and I'll lay out dry clothes for you. You are chilled from the hill and the journey back. There will be tea and sandwiches laid out while you change."

"But it's an emergency. I have to get there at once. . . ."

"That Duchess is well able to cope. Go and get your bath and change. Not much point in getting there looking like a drookit rat. There's your health to think of. If you won't, I will."

She was waiting for him when he emerged, wolfing the sandwiches.

"Take your time! You can finish the last ones in the car. And by the way, I have spoken to the Duchess. She will have a hot whisky toddy waiting for you. If you get boozed up, one of the gamekeepers will run you home." She pushed a car coat over his shoulders.

Raeburn shrugged submissively, making for the door. "Is there no escape?" he heard himself saying.

She said, "None at all."

In the few minutes it took him to cover the road to Kintalla Castle, he realized that he was already restored. The cold stiffness he had brought back from the hills had been replaced by some sense of well-being, and he caught himself smiling wryly at the idea of the several women who were bullying him for his own good, as they imagined. Moreover, it was true that the Duchess was doubtless in command.

He had known her as the young sister of his old rugby-playing mate Bandy Haddo. Somehow in the course of her brief career as a free-lance cookery expert—boardroom lunches, confidential country seminars, and so on—she had encountered the Duke and he had lost no time in marrying her and in begetting a child, a ducal son and heir, upon her. Neither male was, it seemed, in residence at Kintalla.

The castle door was opening as Raeburn ran up the steps, and a man was welcoming him.

"It's yourself, Mr. Raeburn. I'm Fletcher, a kind of butler. Man, but you're very like your pictures. Her grace . . ." But Edith stood just inside the door, and she came at once to his arms.

"Edith—poor Edith," he was saying. "I should have been here long ago."

She held him off, smiling. "But you weren't, and we managed. Now not a word out of either of us until noggin time has well and truly started."

She put him into a great leather chair, in a room off the main hall, and the warm tumbler was in his hand. She said, "Two big gulps—then we'll talk." He downed the draught and said, "Listening."

She was seated too, graceful as ever, the eyes bright, the red hair flaming. "In fact, Barry, I think you know all of it already, but it might do both of us good to have something of a recap.

"Lord Melfort turned up here fairly late last night. He told me he was going to pay you a call, and I assume he did. I can tell you he was seething with anger—not just the usual superior sulks he stages from time to time. He was in no mood to explain anything, and of course I didn't ask. He gave orders for dinner to be served to them in the suite.

"Much later he came downstairs and got somebody to phone for Reid and Macfarlane—you know, the gillies.

"Anyway, they spent a long time talking in the gun room, and when our men went away, Lord Melfort went straight upstairs. I spoke to Reid on the phone, and he told me that his lordship was going out to the moors about eight o'clock the next day—that's this morning—and that he had a rendezvous somewhere with the gillies at nine o'clock. Melfort was away before I was up and about. The next thing I knew they were carrying his body into the courtyard."

"How awful for you!"

"I suppose so. First thing I did was to phone you, but you were away. So it was on to the police, and they sent a senior team out at once, including the police surgeon who made a certification. Statements in full from Reid and Macfarlane and the rest of us. Did you know that Reid's cousin is the deputy chief constable? He said that they don't need any more evidence. There will be an inquiry later, but it's not likely they will trouble us here anymore. I told them that you had seen him the night before, but they didn't think you would be asked to make a statement."

"My God, poor you! You have been at it all day."

"Well, mostly. Anyway, the next thing was to phone the Duke in Paris."

"I should think so. What did he say?"

"You know him. Not a tremor of emotion. If he was a normal man, I should say there was a faint note of relief. But, Barry, is he efficient! At once he mentioned ten things I hadn't thought about, and even the police hadn't thought of some of them. I got some sorting out done, and before he got off the phone I managed to get in a word to ask about the baby. It seems he's fine."

For a moment her face was pinched with grief, for the Duke had taken the baby away so that he might be brought up in France.

Raeburn looked down at his hands until the small sobs had finished.

She went steadily on. "In a very few minutes I had Sir Geoffrey Ballantine, the organization's chief lawyer, on the phone. I asked all the right questions. He was back again in half an hour, and in that time he had spoken to the police, instructed the local undertaker, briefed Melfort's lawyer, and talked to Reid and Macfarlane. By the way, he is full of praise for those two. Says they acted with great decency and consideration, and were quite cool about the wound, which was ghastly—the whole belly was blown out.

"Oh, and another thing," she said. "Sir Geoffrey came up with the idea that I should have someone here as a kind of companion to help me over the present stresses. I imagine this came from the Duke. But I said no. I'm better off on my own. I'm used to it."

By this time she was curled up in her deep chair, shoes off, her legs under her. So that when the real tears came at last she was hardly vulnerable; he kept watching her for the few minutes that the bout lasted, not essaying to touch her or to speak. When she finished, he gave her a fresh handkerchief.

"Sorry about that, Barry. Silly me."

"You'll be the better for it. Okay now?"

"Okay. Thanks. Thanks."

"Things still to do," he told her. "For example, what about"—he motioned to the ceiling—"her?"

"God! The tart," she exclaimed. "I'd forgotten about her, I'm delighted to say. . . . Well, quite a story there. One of the first things I did when they brought home what was left of him was to summon the inamorata from her couch to break the news. She took it like a stoic, mentioning only that this changed things and that she would have to do some planning. Not a word about wanting to view the remains, or showing interest in any of the grisly necessities, which she was happy to leave to me. She ordered the usual hearty lunch, made a few phone calls . . ."

"The fallback," he suggested.

"A well-chosen description. Later she told me that she would have a few hours' shut-eye—her very words—then she would pack and leave. She ordered the car for about now. They came in a Rolls with chauffeur."

"Might it not be a good idea to have a look at what she is packing?" Raeburn asked.

"Barry—I should have thought of that. Of course. Let's go. Upstairs and turn right."

The suite was strewn with clothes, with a woman busy in the midst of them. "Come in," she said. "Make yourselves at home. I'm taking off for the city in half an hour or so—if that suits everybody. In fact, whether it does or not." Looking them over coolly, she nodded in the direction of Raeburn and addressed herself to the Duchess. "Who's he?"

"His name, Miss Pender," was the reply, "is Mr. Barry Raeburn, an old family friend. He is the headmaster of Markland School."

"I was just hoping he wasn't another cop—plainclothes this time. It wouldn't have been wise to bring them in again. . . . Talking of clothes"—she was rummaging and spreading and folding all the time—"I must say, his lordship had some lovely stuff. Look at the quality—pure silk shirts and pyjamas . . ."

They stood in silence for a time, until Edith said, "Are you taking all his effects with you?"

Miss Pender, still busy, replied, "He had no relations, so you might as well consider me as the widow."

Raeburn said, "A merry one, I'll be bound."

"Right you are," she said. "I'll probably hole up in London for a few days—in the flat, of course. He had the keys in his pocket. Sorry about the mess in the washbasin—lot of blood somebody will have to clean up. What he was wearing—kind of shredded—but I was able to salvage the cuff links—bloody job—gold and rubies. He had a lot of money on him—and a lot more in one of the drawers . . . more cuff links, tie pins, two watches, two private telephones, and a whole lot more little treasures that he won't have any use for. . . . I tell you, there's nothing like being an heiress. . . . Oh, by the way, don't be bothered helping me down with the bags. I'll send the driver up for them."

Downstairs again, Raeburn and his hostess sat and looked at each other. She said, "It could even be funny, if . . ."

He said, "Yes, if only. Don't worry. There is nothing we can do, and it's nearly over."

They waited until there were footsteps on the stairs, and the heaving of bags and the closing of the great hall door. Edith was breathing with relief when the telephone rang.

"Yes, of course—put him on. . . . Ah, yes, Mr. Molyneaux. How far are you in the picture about this terrible business? . . . Yes, I imagine that Sir Geoffrey has given you the details, but if you care to go over them now, I shall add anything that you think might be useful." She took time to cover the receiver, saying to Raeburn, "Melfort's lawyer." He could hear the steady professional voice at the other end in a remote drone that went on evenly for minutes. After a time she said, "Mr. Molyneaux, that quite covers everything I know, but you may want to ask questions."

She listened, and then said, "Yes, there were a few calls from newspapers earlier, but I referred them in each case to the police." The lawyer was speaking again, and she answered, "She left a few minutes ago, apparently bound for London, with Lord Melfort's car and chauffeur. . . . She was not, I am bound to tell you, in any sense a normal guest of this house."

There was some further conversation. She said, "There is someone here who might be able to describe better than I can the circumstances. He is Mr. Barry Raeburn, headmaster of Markland School. Would you care to speak to him?"

She handed him the telephone.

"Raeburn," he said.

The precise voice at the other end said, "John Molyneaux. Let me say at once that I know of your connection with Kintalla, and your name has come up occasionally in my late client's papers. I may say that I am much relieved that you have been able to stand by her grace at this shocking time, although I gather that she is very composed."

"The worst is over. How can I help you?"

"Can you fill me in on any hints dropped by Miss Pender about her immediate plans? I shall have some arrangements to make at this end."

"She intends to go immediately to Lord Melfort's London flat and make that her base."

"This gives us time to have the locks changed. The chauffeur will be instructed to garage the car, hand over the keys, and await instructions. He was Lord Melfort's employee, and his wages will be continued for a time. What about the deceased's effects?"

"All neatly packed, I gather, and borne away by herself—in triumph, it would appear . . ."

"Including . . ."

"Including such personal effects as watches, jewels, clothes, and money—a good deal of it, as she announced. You will be doing something about that, I suppose."

"You may be sure. We shall have two detectives waiting at the entrance to the flat—mildly intimidating people from the local headquarters. She will no doubt agree to accompany them to the police station. I take it that you will not want to know the outcome of these investigations?"

"You may want to advise the Duchess in due course." Raeburn hesitated. "Do you think there will be others turning up to make claims?"

"No doubt. But it has been all arranged. I dispose of a small fund with the instructions that any woman who appeared, claiming to have been on intimate terms with the deceased, should be given without question the sum of fifty pounds on condition that a document is signed declaring that no further claims would be made in any circumstances."

"Ingenious, if I may say so."

"You may. It was my idea, in the interest of my client. He was reluctant for many years to make a will, on the grounds that he thought it most unlikely he would ever die.

"We long ago gave up the search for any relatives. I can tell you, for it will be public knowledge very shortly, that all of his considerable fortune will go to his old college in Cambridge in the form of scholarships for people of promise who want to enter some form of public service. Something like the Rhodes fund."

"I take it that I may tell the Duchess about all this."

"Certainly. You have been most helpful. I shall not distress the Duchess any further. Good-bye and thank you."

When he had repeated the salient facts, Raeburn said, "I'll see myself out, Edith," but she came with him.

"You used to have some sort of butler here," he said.

"He's gone. Mutual agreement. The man who let you in is Murdo Fletcher—ex-army. He lives in the lodge house at the main gate. And Reid and Macfarlane are never far away. I'm well protected."

He eased the car up the gentle rise to the main gate, slowing to hear the sound of a violin. After waiting for a while, he got out and lifted the knocker on the oak door. Fletcher came out.

"Mr. Raeburn, it's yourself. Come in and tell me what ye make of it." In the big chairs in front of the fire, they discussed the death of Lord Melfort. It allowed Raeburn to mention his concern for Edith's safety.

Fletcher said, "I tell ye, there's naebody will come near her while I'm aboot—" He pointed to the shotgun on its hooks above the fireplace. "But what sort of hospitality is this? A dram, maybe—or a cup of tea?"

"I like the smell of what's in that pot at the side of the fire. Is there enough for two?"

"That there is. Ye never ken wha wad drap by. I aye tak porridge for ma supper."

"Fine habit. I started it in school a year ago. A good thing at night."

They ate, and Fletcher said, "Here was I sittin' ma lane haein' a wee bit practice at the fiddle, and in ye cam and welcome."

"Don't let me stop you. Carry on."

The other put down his empty bowl and lifted the violin with careful hands. He said, "I was tryin' one of Niel Gow's compositions. It's in three flats. Man, thon's a bugger o' a key. We'll leave it the now. Have ye maybe a favourite pipe march I could gie ye to get me back to my rhythm?"

"I wouldn't mind hearing 'Leaving Lunga.'"

Raeburn listened while the musician played the tune twice. "Thanks. Great!"

"I see ye're a piper yersel'."

"How?"

"Your fingers were doin' the notes on the bars of your chair. Were ye guid at it?"

"I was in the school pipe band when I was a student. Afraid I was no MacCrimmon."

"That's enough modesty. You have a guid straight finger. I expect that if ye are world-famous at something, a lot of folk will be thinkin' ye are no dam guid at anything else."

Raeburn took to the road at last.

"Safe hame, then," said Murdo Fletcher at the gate. "Go canny."

4

In the few months that had passed since he became the headmaster, he had often told himself that one of the best times of the week happened when the senior staff met him for coffee in their common room, and the talk was of shared concerns and jests and plans. They had got to know his style by now; relaxed and involved; no way patronising; with that trick of leadership that showed that any worries he might have were trifles compared with their own. They would pour their coffee and pace about, willing to listen to each other by way of rehearsing for their job of teaching, since it is essential to listen to the young rather than to talk them down.

A good team, he had come to be convinced. Even the new ones he had brought in had quickly fallen into the style. Often, after about ten minutes, he would lead the conversation to some common point of debate, when they would all have their say, if they had a contribution, or else be silent and listen. Strangers visiting, if they appeared to be congenial, were always asked to join this three-times-a-week morning session. Today there was a well-informed journalist in the gathering, and he was moving freely among them.

Shortly before the half-hour was over, Jo Anne Stevenson, his secretary, slipped quietly through the pack and came to Raeburn's side. "A visitor," she said.

"Who?"

"Joan Ker. Here she is." And Joan Ker was standing in the open doorway, looking at them all.

Raeburn's emotion took only the smallest pause and then

surged like a flood over him. For, like no other woman in his
life, he owed her more than anyone else. She had been a teacher
at Markland when he had first come there stricken in health.
When he had been made headmaster, she had insisted on leaving. "No, I must, Barry," she had said. "At least until you get
into your stride here. Maybe we can see about personal things
later. Don't wheedle. I'm sure I've got this right." And because
she had got so many other things right, he had let her go.

Making his way to her across the floor, he noticed that somehow she seemed smaller, almost frailer. He took her hands for a
moment, and they were cold. Raeburn and Joan smiled and did
not speak.

There were hearty greetings, though, from all round the
room. Furness, the head of English, boomed, "Why, if it isn't
old Junior Maths, come back to join the gang."

"Are you coming back, really, Joan? Is she, headmaster?"

"Never mind the 'headmaster'! This is the age of democracy
—we are all equals now—some more than others."

"Hold on a minute." This was Ian Rankine, cutting in good-
humouredly. "I think we should stop hustling the headmaster—
and of course we should give dear Joan a chance to speak for
herself."

Raeburn had a sudden pang, seeing Joan's white face and
watching her gather herself to speak to her old colleagues. She
smiled broadly, saying, "Thanks so much, all of you. No, I'm not
scheduled to turn up here again in the near future. I've got a job
in a distinguished school far from here where they regard themselves as in fierce opposition to Markland, believe it or not."

"Shame," said somebody, and they all laughed.

"But I was visiting in the neighbourhood and thought you
would let me look in . . ."

"No problem!" Rankine seemed to have taken over. "And
welcome as always—in the hope that you may find your way
back here one day."

"Talking of Junior Maths," said somebody, "does she know about young Michael Mackay?"

"That I do. Your latest whiz kid is the talk of the academic world far from here. I think," Joan said, "you will let me take a tiny bit of credit. By the time he was eleven years old, he had me lost in mathematical theories. . . ."

They were laughing as they dispersed. Raeburn stood by her side to watch them go. She said to him, "Got to see you, Barry. Privately. Won't take long."

In his office he took her in his arms. Standing there silently, he had not remembered that she was so little. For a while they did not speak.

At last she moved gently away from him, releasing herself and pushing him away. She whispered, "Not here, dear Barry. Not now. I have things to tell you. Give me a minute to think."

She sat curled into one of the big armchairs, and he surveyed her from his own. He would hear her story in a moment, but now everything in his mind was swamped by the memory of what had been between them. It was at the time of the kidnapping of the Duke's infant son, when the two of them had played perhaps the main part. There was the night they had spent together in the cave at Hewson Dod, before the last act of the rescue. And in that time they had each been rescued and released from a long, solitary imprisonment of the flesh, and had joined in ecstasy. His mind clung to the thought of it as if it were sacred. And here she was. . . .

"I'd better get it over with, Barry. It's bad news. Please don't interrupt. It'll be all the sooner finished. . . ." There was the slightest pause, and she went on. "You remember I stayed with you for the weeks you were in hospital, after the operation by the Duke's specialist from Zurich. I can't describe how gloriously happy I am to see you so well recovered. Anyway, as you know, we parted then for good tactical reasons, as I saw it. You had to get settled, and I got the job I have now. It was soon after that I realized that I was carrying your child."

Raeburn started forward, but she raised a hand and he was silent.

"Barry, you will never know—how can you?—how immensely happy I was in the few weeks that followed. I had it all planned. Everything. I'd have the child and start it on the way in life—the greatest job I could ever have looked for. When the time came, he would be yours, if that is what you still wanted."

"But, of course—and he! He!"

"Yes—he it was. Was. Please let me finish. Not long now . . . I was near my term when I realized there was something badly wrong. With me. Inside. Dr. Grigor took a serious view of the whole thing and had me up to Ayr Hospital. The boss there got in touch with the Duke—"

"The Duke! Of course."

"—and the Zurich man turned up in double-quick time. All this fuss for wee Joan Ker, of whom nobody had ever heard."

"You should have let me know."

"Don't say that, or I'll cry before I finish. It seems I was far gone. First thing to do was to take away the baby, who was badly affected. A boy, they told me. He would never have made it. Then they worked on me, hounded on, poor devils, by the Duke. Too late. Nothing could be done. That's the story. Finished. Like me."

"The Duke. I'll get on to the Duke right away—"

"Don't! Everything possible has been done. He's furious. Looks on it as some kind of personal failure. You can talk to him if you must, but not while I am here. Let me go first. . . . Oh, Barry dear, I am so sorry. Let you down. Lost your son and . . ."

This time he held her until her quiet sobs stopped and they were both able to speak again. Many of her sentences were common sense, and about the future where she would have no part.

"Look after yourself, Barry. Don't do anything too strenuous. No late nights at the desk. There will be another sort of Joan somewhere—luckier. Somebody to nag you kindly. No, I have to go. Well, there's a call on a lawyer chap, other people to see, letters to write, all that. Kiss me now. Not outside at the door. Mustn't be seen taking a fond farewell of an old flame at the front door of the school. People would start to talk. Let me go, man."

He saw her down the steps and into her car. Dry-eyed, she gave a small smile as he waved. She didn't look back.

He rushed back into the office, sweeping up the telephone. "Get me the Duke."

"Yes, headmaster. Do you know where he is—Paris, Vienna, New York, Rome—"

"No, I don't. Just get him for me. Get him now." He put down the phone with a slam and felt ashamed at once. In less than a minute he had lifted the phone again. "I'm sorry about that, Jo Anne."

"Not to worry, headmaster."

"It occurs to me that the Duke's London office will tell his whereabouts, knowing it's an urgent call from me."

"They tell me he is in Rome, and I've put the call through. While we're waiting, can I ask you a question?"

"I suppose so."

"It's about Joan Ker. There's something wrong there. She wouldn't say anything to me, but I hoped you might know. I liked her—everybody liked her. Do you know—what's the trouble?"

"I can't say anything just now, but I promise to tell you soon."

"Suppose that'll have to do. Here's the Duke on now. He's been called out of a meeting. Over."

"Raeburn." It was a statement, not a query. The same implacable, hateful voice to whose owner he owed his life. The Duke was famous—least of all for being a Duke, but for his unstoppable success in every one of the business undertakings he had inaugurated about the world. A man of no emotion, who burned with the terrible ambition for power. Dangerous, ruthless, certain of the rightness of his own decisions.

"Sorry to interrupt. I'm told you have had to leave a meeting."

"Correct. But no doubt you are not phoning on some minor matter."

"It's desperately important. About Joan Ker, the teacher."

"Ah, Miss Ker. Of course. Who has told you about her condition?"

"She left me minutes ago. Came here to tell me about her illness. What can we do about that—now?"

"I am sure she has told you nothing can be done. I am afraid that is final and that her time is very short. You should know that the symptoms are quite different from those in your case, which were capable of being dealt with. Dr. Sanger from Zurich tells me there is only one conclusion—terminal. Perhaps six months earlier he might have been able—but there is no point in speculations of this sort, I am sorry to say.

"I assume you have a special interest, and this does not surprise me. You may say, with truth, that this does not concern me. But I have been concerned."

"It's a terrible tragedy . . ."

"True. Be assured of my sympathy, which will not be of much use to you at this time. Apart from that, you may be disposed to recall at a later stage that my main sentiment is one of anger at the delay in seeking expert knowledge. But then of course the world is full of inefficiencies. Perhaps we can leave the matter there, since discussion will not advance the case where the best medical wisdom has failed."

Raeburn said, "I ought to thank you for forcing it to try."

"No need. . . . Is there anything you want to tell me about the school?"

"Not really. We are on an even keel at the moment. You have been very generous in the matter of the junior technical department."

"Not I. As you know, the Duchess is in possession of almost unlimited funds for that project, and they may be drawn as needed. You might find it helpful to be aware that these funds are strictly earmarked for the Markland scheme and cannot be deployed for any other purpose. In this way I keep control of the resources."

"But—" Raeburn was suddenly appalled at the casual disposal. "Your wife. Surely—"

"She has no substantial sums for her unconditional use. There is a clothing allowance, and household bills and wages are dealt with by a local accountant. Minor matters come under the same control. You have much to learn, Raeburn, about money management."

"So she is a prisoner, then?"

"That would not be my description. She has her choice of many houses, but she prefers Kintalla. The school has been a hobby, in a sense."

"But she is lonely. She is missing the child dreadfully."

"I have to be the judge as to what is best for the child. He is heir to a great inheritance and must be prepared for it. All this is, of course, wide of your responsibility, but you may be interested to learn that I have been compiling a list of the names he will carry—outside of the titles, I mean."

"For his christening?"

"I have said nothing about rites, although there may be some long-term advantage in conforming to the modes of, say, France or Italy. These are flexible matters at our level. As you perhaps know, we have for centuries been Anglican in England and Presbyterian in Scotland, a style adopted not many years ago by the British royal family."

"Your lot thought of it first?"

"As with most things. I will try to tell you about the child's names. In my house there are many to choose from, but I have decided that, when the time comes, there will be included in the list the name of Raeburn."

"Mine! Good God, why?"

"Because we are in your debt in the matter of the kidnapping.

I take it that you have no objection. In fact, it is too late for objections, for the matter has been registered with the various Colleges of Heralds. It may gratify you to know that, in time to come, people will enquire as to how that name comes to be coupled with our name, and you will be mentioned, not without honour."

There was no getting away from the staggering surprise of this chilly fellow, who at this stage might even be thought to be enjoying the conversation. *What the hell do I say next?* Raeburn was thinking, when the Duke went on.

"I must also commend you for the support you gave in the case of the death of Lord Melfort. I know all the details."

"A bad show. We haven't heard the last of that."

"I believe you may be wrong. The Scottish legal procedures do not tend to dramatise these blunders."

Raeburn was gathering his ideas to make some final point when the remote voice at the other end came: "Raeburn, I think we have exhausted all the topics on which we may have a mutual interest. If you call me again, I shall assume it is on a matter of large importance."

Raeburn had organised the school curriculum so that he still did some teaching, and his next class was about to start. He made a point of being at his desk before the bell. The routine gave him a brief moment to gather his thoughts and put to the back of his mind the news about Joan Ker. He knew that later in the day the reality would hit him, but now he had to deal with the fresh faces that were waiting, all of which would in time have to hold up against the kind of grief that was making his heart and belly cold. So he toiled his way through the subject that was his specialty, the lessons of history and how they might be applied to correct the human attitude, which learns so little from what has gone before.

In the afternoon he took time to clear his desk, and then set off with the visiting journalist to make the rounds of the build-

ings and the grounds. The journalist's questions were more en-
lightened than most, making the time spent more bearable.

At last he saw the man into his car and off down the main
drive. He was able at last to walk the grounds alone with his sick
heart, letting the pain of the other parting that was soon to come
flow through him in a sullen, deadening flood. How long—the
old predicament again—how long would he be fated to go this
solitary road, when he had pondered with pleasure the prospect
of a shared journey, and Joan Ker at the heart of it? He forced
aside the selfishness that was making him feel sorry for himself,
when he should be praying for her. This he did, thinking the
muddled words as he went.

Walking a path that bordered the football pitches, he heard
the familiar sound of a football being kicked. When he pushed
through the trees, he found young Michael Mackay alone on one
of the minor pitches, kicking the ball up and down the touchline.

"What's going on?" Raeburn had moved forward from the
trees.

Young Mackay was in no way abashed. He gathered the ball
and came up. "I'm practising a new tactic. We have the matches
next Saturday against Glendochart—seniors, and the under-sixteens. I'm the captain of Markland under-sixteens."

"I know that. Who do you think appointed you?"

"You did, sir. Very much obliged. Well, we've simply got to
win this one, if only to encourage the senior chaps whose game
comes on after ours. I'm just trying out a wheeze that might
catch them out."

"Good for you! What is it?"

"You can watch if you like," Mackay said.

Twenty more times Mackay, standing two yards from the
touchline, punted the ball downfield, so that it bounced thirty
yards forward and still stayed in play. Raeburn joined in, standing downfield where the ball was landing and punting it back to
the young tactician, who caught it with neat confidence. The
evening light started to fade.

"Time to quit, I think," said Raeburn. "Are you joining us for evening supper?"

"You bet, sir. That's really my breakfast, you know."

"What is on tonight?" he asked as they walked towards the showers. "In the sky, I mean."

"Not much that I can pay attention to, although there is some sort of Russian in the Clyde area. I'm dismantling, actually. Some of those boffins are due in the next few days, before the end of term, and there are some things I don't want them to see."

"Fair enough," Raeburn said.

Somehow he got through the rest of the day. It was hardly first light when his bedside phone rang and he spoke to it.

"Barry—is that you? It's Dick Coulson here."

"Dr. Coulson. What a pleasure. I was hoping it might be someone who could cheer me up. What can I do for you?" Richard Coulson was the former headmaster and founder of Markland School. "Where are you phoning from?"

"From Ayr. Barry, I'm not calling to cheer you up. I'm calling about Joan Ker."

"Oh, yes, I know about Joan."

"Barry, you don't know. She's dead."

5

"She is dead."

Joan Ker dead? It was impossible. He had heard, but it simply could not be believed. He fended off the knowledge with a tremulous bluster. "Say that again, Dr. Coulson. I'm not sure I . . ."

"Joan Ker is dead, Barry."

"But how is that possible? She was here only yesterday."

"To say good-bye, I imagine. If you will listen to me, I'll tell you all I know."

Coulson cleared his throat and then said, "I have been at this since the small hours of the morning. She has been working in Ayr, and I have known for some time that her illness was terminal. She knew it also. She wrote me a letter yesterday telling the whole story and what she meant to do about it. She wrote that she was not sending you a letter and that you would understand. What happened was that she spent yesterday afternoon clearing things up: letter to her lawyer about her will, funeral, people to advise, death notice, all that. One to her only near relative, a married sister in Inverness.

"My letter was delivered early this morning—say four o'clock. What happened was that after nightfall she parked her car in a side street near the mortuary. It was quick work after that. She had a handful of tablets that had been prescribed for her and never used. It must have been over fast. Some time in the night the police got suspicious and forced the car open. She was already gone. A police surgeon certified the death. The letters were found and delivered by hand. There is really no more."

Both men took time to grieve silently, finding no words. It was Raeburn who said at last, "It was nearly an exact copy of my own experience. I blame myself—"

"Don't you dare! I never knew what it was that you had attempted, but I think she did."

"Yes, she did. That's what gave her the idea."

"You realise that this is a blessing. I admire her. One of these days I may even envy her."

"Don't say that! What now, then?"

"Everything looked after, as you would expect. Funeral at eleven next Tuesday morning in the crematorium here. I expect you will want to be there. If you like, I'll write a piece for the school magazine. That's about it, Barry, not much more to be said. I'm so sorry. She said in the letter you were very close."

"She was right. Don't ask me any more."

"I'll never ask you anything you wouldn't want to tell me. But I must say you are the kind of chap who could do with someone to tell things to. Keep it in mind, Barry. I say, that's enough. See you on Tuesday."

In a short time his secretary came in, troubled.

"Headmaster! I have a confession. I listened in to part of your conversation with Dr. Coulson. You know I worked for him here also, before you. This is terrible news."

"You don't need to tell me."

"I want to go away to cry. Do you mind?"

"Not in the least. Drop a tear or two for me."

"I believe I knew her as well as anybody else. She had hardly any people of her own, and she came to work here about the same time as I did, a few years ago. She was good—kind, considerate, thoughtful, all the right things. Before I forget, there was a phone call for you—a man called Mr. Bev Capell—I made him spell it. Said he was representing the interests of the late Lord Melfort and wanted to come and discuss with you matters raised by his lordship in your recent conversation."

"Oh, he does, does he? Get me a call to Mr. John Molyneaux —we spoke the other day, you will have his number."

Moments later Molyneaux was speaking to him. "Mr. Raeburn—let me say at once that matters are working out smoothly at this end in the matter of my late client's affairs. What about you?"

Raeburn told him briefly about the call.

"Familiar as I am with many of the details of his lordship's affairs, I never heard of a Mr. Capell. You may take it that the name is fictitious, although I believe that I may be able to recall a character who might resort to such a cover."

"May I make a speculation about what might be the purpose of this approach?"

"You may not, Mr. Raeburn, if I may presume to give you professional advice. It may be that some aspects of my late client's activities may become the subject of official investigation, and you might find yourself involved. Understood?"

"Completely. I should not welcome that. May I inform you of any important developments, though?"

"Certainly. Without delay. Let us hope there are none. Goodbye, sir."

It was time for Raeburn to turn back to the hundred smallish items that made up the running of the school. One of these was the trip he had arranged for a small school party to travel to the annual rugby international Calcutta Cup game between Scotland and England. It was the oldest international game in existence, and the teams met every year, one time at Murrayfield in Edinburgh, the next year at Twickenham in London. This was Murrayfield's year, and he had ground tickets for a party of twelve. They would travel there in the school minibus, have a meal somewhere on the way, see the game, and leave immediately for the long trip back to Markland. The boys would never forget it, and with an all-important end-of-term game due, they might even see some tricks they could try to carry out on their own playing fields.

The dozen he had selected, with difficulty, would be himself and Ian Rankine, the teacher who shared with him the main football coaching; Calder, the school captain, and Bremner, the captain of the first fifteen; the royal prince, whom they all called David, and his detective; Ballantine, the games master; Briggs Hewitt, the first Markland pupil he had ever met, an abandoned youngster of ten farmed out by parents who didn't want him, and who was now in his teens; Mike Mackay, who was also captain of the junior fifteen; and three other worthy seniors, one of whom might be the dux of the year.

He had also, of course, to go over with Ballantine the arrangements for the Sunday afternoon cross-country run, for the Coulson Cup. Apart from the summer sports meeting in their own grounds, this would be the last of the winter-term events.

Ian Rankine would be driving the bus. Raeburn went early to check on the details, and when he arrived at the bus it was empty except for Elaine Grandison and Frances Allen installed in seats inside.

"What's all this?" asked Raeburn, entering.

The Grandison girl faced him, saying, "Nothing too serious, headmaster. It's just that the two of us have decided to join the party. This is the age of equality, and we are all very democratic nowadays."

"Out!" said Raeburn, pointing to the door. "Out, you two, at once. You know the arrangements, and you have not been included. Leave the bus at once!"

"But, headmaster, we have our rights. You can't—"

"I can do anything here. You have no rights but what you earn. Don't you ever dare again to encroach on them. Outside, I say, and wait on the tarmac."

"It's not fair," she grumbled, rising reluctantly. "This was supposed to be a school of liberal principles, and I don't see any sign of them. I'm going to report this to my father. He will take me away from here."

Even as she made the naive threat, Raeburn knew he should

have let it pass in silence, but he was moved by his anger to say, "Is that a promise, Elaine? It's good news."

She stumbled, sulking, out of the bus and stood beside Rankine. Raeburn stood beside Frances Allen inside and said, "Go quietly, Frances. Go now. There's nothing to be gained by trying to stay. It's not your day, Frances."

At this moment Elaine put her head in the bus door and shouted defiantly, "Anyway, we'll see the whole game on television. Better than you will see it."

He shouted across the space to Ian Rankine, "Ian, get Miss Wilson to me quick."

Before he sped off, Rankine said, "Won't take a minute. She is taking early tennis on the courts."

Pamela Wilson was the tough games mistress, a spinster probably in her early forties who had won international honours for Scotland at both hockey and tennis. She was rumoured to hate men, and most of her girl pupils were inclined to think she also hated females. They could see her now in the distance, outpacing Rankine in a determined run.

In the bus Raeburn stood beside the still seated Frances Allen. "Outside, Frances," he said. "You heard me."

Looking up at him, she seized his jacket sleeve and leaned her head into his arm. In a voice that trembled, she said quietly, "Oh, you! Sir—" She rose and left the bus.

The iron-gray head of Miss Wilson bobbed along the windows of the bus towards the door as he stepped out. She was not even breathing hard. "You sent for me, headmaster?"

"Yes. A sad case of indiscipline here, Miss Wilson. I should like you to deal with it. Elaine and Frances here have fallen out with authority—"

"Surely not!"

"I suggest a most strenuous tennis coaching session starting at two-thirty P.M. and lasting for at least two and a half hours. They must on no account be permitted to watch the rugby game on television, and that goes for repeats later in the day. Okay?"

"With pleasure, headmaster. This way, girls—back up the drive. And see me on the courts at exactly two-thirty."

"I don't think," said Elaine Grandison, "that you'll see *me* there."

Miss Wilson pounced at her. "Silence, Grandison! How dare you! I can promise you solemnly that you will indeed be there. And if there is another item of insolence I shall whack you. March!"

She herded them towards the school, passing the Murrayfield party jogging down towards the bus, with Rankine in their midst. Calder, the school captain, announced breezily, "Bang on time, sir. Have we missed anything?" He gestured after the Wilson party.

"Nothing that need concern you. All aboard!" As they settled in, Raeburn pondered the oddity of the Allen girl's behaviour. There was no time to dwell on it, however. As the bus rolled towards the main gateway and the road north, he said, "We're in no hurry, so we'll take it easy. Stopping to eat just about noon. We'll be travelling through some interesting country. Some of you may know bits of it well. If anybody has anything worth saying about what we can see from the bus, he shouts it out so that we can all hear. Right?"

One of the seniors took it up at once, intoning, "And so we say farewell to that learned institution, Markland School, famed in song and story. . . ." The rest was lost in their laughter. Raeburn relaxed. They were away.

They rollicked and jested all the way, and Raeburn was happy to let them get on with it. Occasionally he had to turn a deaf ear, it being the belief among the young that adults are deficient in hearing, or are short of information about current minor indecencies. But for the most part it was straightforward, and some of it was even witty. The prince's detective, sitting stolidly in the back corner of the bus, took no part in the uproar, since he was engaged in a career where articulation was not one of the professional requirements.

Raeburn sat beside Rankine in the front, and at one point Rankine said, "Tell me about the Wilson showdown. I'll bet she put the fear of God in these two girls. She does that to me too."

"Never admit it, but I know what you mean." And he told Rankine about the dialogue and the sentence of the tennis lessons. They laughed discreetly.

"Ah, well—all in the good cause of discipline," Rankine said. "By the way, watch out for that young Frances Allen. Harmless —but I think she has a crush on you. Eyes and ears on the alert, I always say."

"Don't be daft, Ian."

In good time they arrived at the hostelry, not too far from Edinburgh, where he had arranged the meal. It was a plain restaurant and tearoom with no liquor license, so that none of the seniors and the adventurous could sneak off to a cocktail bar. They gathered round the long table, snatching at hot pies and sausage rolls and great plates of sandwiches and huge sloshing beakers of fruit drinks.

Raeburn tapped a glass for silence. "No need for any kind of formality. Just one or two things for you to remember, and it is the last chance I'll have to tell you. I've arranged for the bus to be parked at a garage a quarter of a mile from Murrayfield, and we'll walk to the grounds together, for if you lose sight of me you won't get in since I have all the tickets. Immediately after the game make your way straight back to the bus—no hanging about—and we shall probably be separated in the crowd.

"We'll be there in good time to see the entertainment on the park before the game. Our seats are on the touchline in the middle of the new stand."

"Sir, do the teams see the entertainment?"

"None of it. They'll be in the dressing rooms below the stand—"

"Shaking—"

"No doubt. Anyway, it'll be a good game. Now, here is one thing I have to impress on you. Don't forget it. Usually after a game finishes, a great mob of people who should know better invades the pitch. That's not for you. Once the first rush out is over, back to the bus—everybody—immediately. We set off for home at once. Any questions? Okay, then—enjoy the game."

He often wondered if there would ever be any end to the endless requirement of explaining and repeating. In a crowd like this there were always those who got it the first time, those who didn't get it, or had to have it repeated by their mates, and those who forgot what was said at once.

Their seats were opposite the team tunnel, so that they would be the first to see the jerseys come out. There were people present who had seen a hundred international games here and who would keep coming until they died. Some of them passed in front of the Markland seats, carrying their tartan knee rugs, waving to friends, often accompanied by tweedy daughters who, in many cases, were the aunts or sisters of the players. There was some great sense of continuity, and most of them felt that without their enthusiasm their team could not hope for victory. It was terribly important that Scotland should win. And yet of all the countries they played in the widening international rugby scene, England somehow remained the hardest to beat.

The bands came to a new formation in front of the main stand to play the national anthem and then to get bundled off swiftly so the game could get started. There was sudden activity at the mouth of the tunnel; civilian men emerged and then turned to wave a signal; then the white flood of the English players swarmed out, looking immense. They scattered to one end of the pitch. The band faltered to the end of some southern musical salute, and the starting drone of the bagpipes was lost in the roar as the blue Scots shirts came out, fanning out to the other end of the ground. There was a minute or two of the galvanic warm-up darting and leaping. Then the players ran to the front of the stand, lining up for the presentation.

A royal personage appeared with the officials and moved along the lines of the players, shaking hands and exchanging the obligatory few words. A senior leaned forward from the Markland rank and said to the prince, "One of your mob." David smiled and nodded tolerantly. The Irish referee in his green jersey looked to the two captains, blew his whistle, and the game was on.

By halftime it was even scoring, and it had not been good rugby. In the end the result hung upon whether the Scottish place kicker could convert, from far out on the touchline, the try that had just been scored in the corner. There was an agony of silence as he dug, set the ball, watched it fall over, set it again, and sent the ball twisting and revolving between the posts to bring the score from one point behind to one point ahead. The double whistle signalled the goal, and immediately the end of the game.

Not a Scot in the crowd was in his seat. Those not behind the barriers rushed for the park and their heroes, with half the Markland party. As Raeburn saw them sprint away, he was on his feet, shouting, "Markland, back here! Markland!" But only the rearmost of his party heard him. One or two of them hesitated for a moment and then rejoined the rush. A few turned back, abashed, and came to the seats.

"Not much we can do now." Rankine's voice tried to be reassuring.

"Oh, Jesus!" It was the prince's detective. "My fellow is in there! What the hell do we do now? What are you going to do about it?" His face was flushing with apprehension.

Raeburn took a deep, steadying breath. "No sense in looking for them in that melee. Some of them will come back, and we'll wait here for a few minutes. The others will make for the bus, and soon we'll do the same. That's it."

"All very bloody well for you. You don't have as much responsibility as some people. . . ."

"Quiet, sergeant! I am in charge of this party. He will come to no harm in that crowd."

" 'In charge,' he says." The detective grumbled his way into the invading crowd, which was eventually dispersing. A few of the Markland boys appeared, until there were only two missing, and one was the prince.

With the pitch almost empty, Raeburn gathered up his flock. "Okay, everybody. Back to the bus. The others know where to come."

The detective was visible ahead of them, striding, glowering and anxious, to the bus, searching as he walked. The boys surged ahead, wriggling past and round other knots of the crowd. Raeburn, recognised on all sides, was stopped several times for autographs and the inescapable reminiscence.

As the crowd thinned ahead of him, he saw he was the last of the Markland party and spurted to catch up. Someone was marching at his side, a quarter pace behind his right elbow. As he veered away to shake him off, he was aware of a figure closing in on his left, until the two men, whom he had not turned to look at, were suddenly alongside and pressing into him. He could feel the hard arm muscles, and was bracing for whatever was to be, when a half-remembered voice said at his right ear, "Aye, that's right, Mr. Raeburn. Just keep going."

And on the other side a voice with the same cadence added, "We'll just talk on the move. There is things to say."

Raeburn's head turned each way only slightly, to make sure they were Reid and Macfarlane, the gamekeeping estate men who knew about some of the Duke's bloodier requirements and had a record of not failing him.

"What's this about, then?" Raeburn asked, hurrying to keep up with them. "Is it something about the prince?"

"Not a bit of it. That fellow will come to no harm. No, it's about Lord Melfort."

"Lord Melfort? That was a bad affair. The Duchess was very grateful for the part you played."

"Like enough. We wouldn't be surprised now if the Duke was grateful too, supposing he was one for the talking." There was a small snort of what might be laughter on either side, and then the other voice said, taking his turn, "We thought that, you being a quiet man as well, you would be better to know it was us who did for him."

"What? What's that? You mean you two killed him?"

"Just so."

"But—but—what in God's name did you do that for?"

"Well, we doubt if you knew the kind of gentleman he was. Would you believe that he came to us and offered us a lot of money . . ."

"Aye—a lot of money. You know what for—"

"For to kill you. He wanted you out of the way, and he would have made it worth our while."

"Now, sir, that wouldn't ever do at all. For one thing, the Duke would have been angry. He would never want a thing to happen to you."

"So there was only one thing to do."

"And that is just what we did."

"So here you are, none the worse. And he's away."

"But like enough he still has some friends. So you'd better be careful."

Raeburn, listening as the improbable dialogue unfolded, asked, "What now?"

"Nothing much. We'll be keeping a weather eye open. . . ."

"And you might be better to go back a different way to the one you came today."

The pressure on his shoulders suddenly eased as the two men strode away from him, their long, tireless hill legs swinging, the faded tweeds moving forward. "Keep in touch," he called, but no answer came back.

There was only one missing when he rejoined his party at the bus. The prince had not arrived.

"There's no end to the trouble there will be about this." The detective's nerve had gone. "I'm calling in the local police. And I have to report to the palace. Through headquarters."

"Give him a few minutes more. There could be all kinds of reasons—"

"I'll get fired. And I'll bloody well see to it that you get fired as well."

6

The detective took a radio transmitter from his jacket pocket. His face had gone from red to off-white. He wrenched the small aerial upright, cleared his throat several times to get his voice going, and started to give some call sign. They all watched.

All but Calder, who tapped the man on the shoulder, was brushed aside, and tapped again. "Sergeant Miller," he said.

At last the sergeant turned on him, glowering. Calder said no word, but with his thumb pointed along the road in the direction behind the detective's back. Miller turned at last and looked.

The prince was walking towards them, waving cheerfully. At his side an enormous youngish man carrying a hold-all walked self-consciously. They joined the group.

"So sorry, sir," the prince said to Raeburn. "Sorry to be late. There is a good explanation. Do you mind, sir, if I give you it in private?"

"I do mind. Give it in public so that we can all hear. You have made every one of us worry about you. And you have twice disobeyed orders. Speak up."

"Oh, I do apologise, sir. I should never have joined the rush onto the field—there was nothing very exciting on the pitch anyway, for the teams seemed to disappear at once. I then thought I should go and pay respects to my relative. I only managed a few words, because I got a fierce telling-off for being on my own. I couldn't get away quickly enough. Then I thought I'd improve the shining hour and even perhaps get a good mark or two by worming my way into the dressing rooms and getting a few interviews for the school magazine. Which I did. Anony-

mous, too." He turned aside to the detective. "Sorry to have
worried you, sergeant. By the way, somebody is trying to talk to
you," for the radio was squeaking with a metallic voice. The man
fumbled with it.

Nothing was going to be serious after this performance, and
Raeburn joined in the laughter. But he said to the prince, "I
suppose that is enough for now, but there will be a private session later. Would you mind presenting us to your guest?"

Laughing again, the prince looked round at them all, saying,
"Does no one recognise him?"

The detective pushed forward, facing the newcomer.

"I don't, for one," he said. "Who are you? Are you police?"

The other looked down at him affably and replied, "No' me.
I'm far too wee. I'm a plumber."

By this time their group was attracting attention, and people
were coming in off the street to gather round and hear what
might happen next.

"Anyone else not know him? Hands up if not." The prince
looked around and pointed to the diminutive Biggs Hewitt.
"You're the youngest. You tell us."

Hewitt gulped, and his ears reddened with embarrassment.
"He's Hughie Beattie, and he plays for Teviotdale. He scored
the first try for Scotland today. That's him. . . . Hughie—eh—
Mr. Beattie."

There was a cheer for this, with more of the crowd moving in
from the street and cries of recognition for the hero of the game
in their midst. The prince said, "I'd better tell you how he comes
to be here—"

Hughie interrupted. "Maybe it would be better if I told you
mysel'. I have to get back to Teviotdale fast. The minute we
came off the pitch at the end of the game, there was an emergency call for me from the toon—the town. I told you I'm a
plumber. Only a one-man business so far, but it will soon be
bigger. Well, I have the contract for the county sewage mainte-
nance, and something has gone wrang wi' the valves on the

outflow. So it's up tae me tae sort it pronto. This young fellow"
—he indicated the prince—"heard about it and said you would
tak' me in the bus and drap me at the toonheid, so I'm fair
hoping it's all right wi' you."

"Absolutely fine. We've a spare seat or two."

"He'll need two to hissel'," said one of the onlookers, who
had by this time raised a cheer, which brought more crowding
in. The story was passing round fast, and the newcomers were
swiftly into the throng with their match programmes held out for
autographs. The prince was included in the celebrities who had
to sign, as some schoolboy who had briefly touched the skirts of
great events.

Raeburn got them sorted out at last and aboard, to great
cheering from the assembly. As he ushered Beattie into the bus,
the big forward said, "You'll no' mind me, Mr. Raeburn—Barry
—you refereed a game I was playing for the south juniors a
while ago."

"I mind it well. You were playing lock forward, the same as
today. And you scored a try then too."

"I hope we didnae let ye doon the day either."

Beattie turned out to be a hilarious addition to the party. He
knew all their songs, and they got to know some of his. And they
probed for gossip from the great games in which he had fea-
tured. Michael Mackay sat beside him for a time, busy with some
problem about the rules of the game of rugby, and at one time
was drawing some maneuvre on the back of his programme and
pressing the player for his opinion about the feasibility of the
move.

"Aye, I think that would work, lad. I don't see why it
shouldnae'."

Somebody asked him about the traditional party after the
match. "Are you sorry you're missing it?"

"No' that much. I'm lucky, for I've been at quite a few. I tell
you, I think I'm safer here than back thonder. Like enough I'll

hae tae work a' night, but come the mornin' I'll no' hae a sair heid like the maist o' thae ithers."

They dropped him at the head of the High Street in the old town of Teviotdale and cheered him away. "Good plumbing!" someone had shouted after him, and the others took up the cry.

"Come and see us anytime if you find yourself near Markland," Raeburn had said to him. The reply had been, "I might just dae that. I have a wee private contract at Kintalla Castle. My auld freen Murdo Fletcher lives in the gatehouse there, and the estate is putting in a new bathroom for him."

Later Raeburn made the rounds of the senior common rooms, where the Saturday night coffee parties were busy. His bleeper called, and he heard the voice of Mrs. Gibson, the housekeeper.

"Telephone, headmaster. Important."

In his office he said to the telephone, "Raeburn here."

A cool female voice acknowledged him. "Ah, Mr. Raeburn. The Palace here. Will you please speak with the Lord Chamberlain."

"Certainly." He drew a writing pad towards him and got ready with the pen.

"Mr. Raeburn?"

"Yes, my Lord Chamberlain. Raeburn speaking."

"Good evening. I am glad to have a word with you. All's well with the school, I am sure?"

"Set fair, I should say. We are running up to end of term."

"Lucky chap. There's no end of term here. . . . Well, my boss has asked me to convey an urgent message to you. Unable to speak personally because of state business here tonight, but of course you will receive a letter shortly. It has been decided that the prince will leave Markland almost at once and will be posted to that Canadian school that has been discussed before. The detective will make the travel arrangements. It is hoped that this will not disturb any schemes you have in mind."

"Not at all. As you know, I have already recommended the move."

"That was taken into consideration. I have to convey also a message of gratitude for the attention you have given the prince."

"To tell the truth, he's just been one of the chaps here."

"Has he kept in line?"

"Reasonably well. One of my last chores will be to reprimand him for stepping out of line this very day. Nothing too serious."

"Fine. Lay it on good and heavy—he can't get too much in the way of reminders."

After hanging up, Raeburn buzzed the senior common room and found the prince was there. "Tell him to report to me at my office without delay." That was all that was needed. Shortly he was saying, "Come in," to the tentative tap at the door.

The prince was there, entering deferentially. He stood opposite the desk and at once spoke. "I hope you will allow me, sir, to offer a most sincere apology for the events of this afternoon."

Raeburn let him fall silent for a moment and told him, "Before we launch into any apologies, perhaps we had better look at the reason for them. You heard me give a specific order and you flouted this order. Furthermore, you stayed away, causing great concern to us and especially to Sergeant Miller, who is charged with your safety. Do you realise that this action put his career in jeopardy? Answer me."

The lad stammered. "Believe me, sir, I—I have given it serious thought. I have already apologised to Miller, and hope you will allow me—to—to—"

Raeburn let him flounder on and at last waved his stumbling words aside. "David," he said, "you are in a situation where the ordinary formalities of an apology will never make up for the offence. Never. There is no point in pretending that you are an ordinary pupil or that the ordinary disciplines will cover you or ever will. You and your family have been set aside to carry out duties far beyond the understanding of the rest of us. I greatly regret that my last task as your headmaster is to hand you this lecture. At the same time, the best impression you can leave here with is to remember what I have said."

There were a few tears now, and Raeburn suddenly smiled at him, saying in a softer voice, "But you know, if you do the job well, there are privileges too.

"Now, I have another point to make. Sit down, David."

He told him briefly about the Canadian posting. The prince listened gravely, knowing that he was already into a life where he would have few personal choices.

"I shall be sorry to leave here, sir," he said.

"Life consists of leaving things behind. My God, David, what a cliché! Forget I said it, but you'd do well to remember what it is about." And so they parted.

Raeburn began to relax; his first move was to pour himself a steep dram of malt whisky. He performed the act like a minor sacrament, caressing the crystal goblet in a practised hand, then holding it up near his eye so that he could recognise the ornamental line of the cut glass where the golden liquor should reach. Then came the measuring of the cold water. He settled into his chair and reached for a familiar book. After a time he put the book aside, preferring to sit and think about Joan Ker.

There was a tap on his door, firm but not loud. Opening it, he found Pamela Wilson standing there.

The games mistress was wearing a tweed jacket and skirt in a cloudy check. He couldn't remember having seen her in a skirt before—possibly at Sunday church service?—her normal wear being trouser suits that had seen strenuous usage. He was absorbing this information when he realised that they had not spoken. This set him to grinding out what might have looked like a grin of welcome, when she spoke.

"It's me, headmaster," she said. "Can you be bothered?"

"No bother at all." It was meant to sound warm and hearty. "Come in and welcome."

She sat in the chair opposite his, gathering her limbs with

athletic elegance, and spoke at once. "I thought I ought to let you have some kind of a report on the discipline session."

"Good idea. I hope it worked out all right. But first—I generally enjoy a comforting dram about this time. What will you have?"

"Brandy, thank you."

He groped for a balloon glass and poured a good drink. She sat for a moment, cupping it.

"So?" he said.

"All went according to plan. I gave those two young women the workout of their lives. Never a moment's rest for the two full hours. There was the occasional protest and a sob or two, but they were too cowed to do anything but obey orders. Not much talent there, though, so Wimbledon has been spared another couple of duffers. They probably ended up hating tennis for life, which is another blessing. And they were so exhausted they fell into bed, and they will no doubt still be there by morning."

"No rough stuff?"

"None at all. Grandison paraded right on time, so that the threats never came to anything."

"Thank God for that. I was terrified you had come to make some confession."

"Not to worry—not this time. By the way, the word must have got around that there might be a public whacking on the cards, and we had quite a little audience of expectant boys. Your young male is an inveterate voyeur." She took a deep, satisfied swallow of the brandy, and they shared what was, for him at least, a relieved laugh.

After a time she asked, "By the way, how was the game?" So he told her about the game; in fact, he told her about everything that had gone on that day, and other matters about the school, as the realisation came to him that she was easy to talk to.

He brought her back to the game, saying, "I hope you didn't want to see it on television."

"Not to worry—part of the job."

"Still, I'm sorry. For all I know, you may be an old Murrayfield fan."

"You could call me that."

"What was the reason? Should I know?" He poured them fresh drinks and after a time, looking into her glass, she said, "Better to say, *who* was the reason."

He nodded, looking at her directly. This was what she had been wanting to tell him. "Tell me. Anybody I know?"

She gave him again a level, fearless look and took a minute to speak. At last she said the name of a player who had in his day been almost as famous as Raeburn himself.

He repeated the name. "Him!" He was amazed. "But—I knew him well. Didn't he . . . ?"

"Yes—killed. Northern Ireland."

For the moment he had forgotten that the man was in the army and had been posted to Ireland with his regiment. That useless bloody war. Well, weren't they all. . . . It had been quite a story at the time, but the memory of it was fading, mingling with so many other disasters.

He gathered up some thoughts about sorrow, but they sounded thin as he spoke them, and he let them drift to silence.

She let the silence hang for a little, then said, "Of course I could be wrong, but I wanted you to know. Difficult to guess if things should be told or not. . . . I wanted you to know because of the news about Joan Ker."

"What specially about Joan Ker?"

"Oh, Barry—everybody knew about Joan Ker—about you both. Everybody down there, I mean." She nodded in the direction of the staff common room. "They were all in favour, if that means anything to you. She would have been ideal back here."

"That was to be the plan."

"Bad luck. Well, that's how it goes. Sorry, I don't mean to sound so casual, but you know—of course you know. . . ."

"How did you cope?"

"My case is different. He was my only—episode—for life. So I set out to invent another character for myself: the professional spinster, hard as nails, away with emotion, no time for man nor beast. Wizened and withering, fairly efficient but something of a figure of fun. For me, it was the only way I could cope. That's not your path."

"I can see only one way ahead now—"

"Of course, the school. You'll go on giving it all you've got, and you will turn out to be a great headmaster. But only because there will be more to your life than that. You haven't the temperament to be a loner. Barry, for God's sake, get somebody. That's all. You have had enough of me Barry-ing away at you. No—don't show me out."

She closed the door behind her.

He sat in the chair, and the thoughts rambled in his head, without shape or coherence. At last he reached for the bottle.

7

On Sunday morning, the next day, more than half the school, in running gear or track suits, had gathered for the morning job of two laps round the grounds. All the girls seemed to be in the assembly, as were all the senior boys; they knew it would be a fast-paced trot, and Raeburn would be leading it.

It was difficult for Raeburn to tell, among the innumerable exercises and events and classroom occasions and small tutorials and sports peaks and the cherished trivia of his life—it was difficult to tell what might be the most enjoyable. But he liked this morning trot on the grounds that were the home of all of them, and in a strange way he had come to feel that there would be some who might remember these runs better than the history and grammar and limping scientific basics that they had been sent to Markland to absorb.

Rankine would be taking the junior boys on a more modest jog of a mile or so. But his lot had already launched into the ancient jests that go inevitably with such runs. Raeburn took no part in the badinage, except to smile occasionally and to laugh if anything original emerged, which was rarely. After a short time the lines came, like the worn pages of an old script. Threadbare jokes about the quality of the school food, obscure references to the habits of girls, and the inelegant postures they assumed when running, or indeed when doing anything. Some of the girls tried repartee. And soon they were in sight of the finish.

The juniors had already arrived. Instead of dispersing to their morning showers, they had gathered round a tall figure. Before Raeburn could identify the newcomer, one of the seniors shouted, "It's Dr. Coulson!" And they swept faster over the last stretch.

Dr. Coulson had been the founder of Markland, and its only headmaster until he had appointed Barry Raeburn scarcely a year before. Raeburn and he waved to each other across the heads, and Coulson turned back to the throng. He had seen most of them grow up under his care; now he took time to say the right things, ask the right questions, and be unpatronisingly amazed at the maturity with which twelve months had endowed them.

At last he said, "Right, men—and ladies. Allow me to pay my respects to the headmaster."

They talked in Barry's study room, first through the open door of the small shower room and then in the great chairs. He began with apologies. "Of course it's unforgivable, Barry, but I was seized with a notion to watch the cross-country race and even, if you will allow me, to present my old pot to the winner. . . ."

"Delighted! You must know there is nobody more welcome here than you are."

"The lads were splendid. Most of them look pretty adequate. I must say I was taken with the style of your young ladies. One of your best innovations."

"Glad you think so. You might call it the thin end of the wench. They are a handful, of course. I worry about doing it all the right way."

"Don't! There is no right way. How could two old bachelors be expected to solve problems that have baffled wise men since time began? By the way, I can tell you I am not going to infest the school. There's nothing so ex as an ex—"

"We can have lunch here and talk."

"Forgive me, but I have a better offer. I was in touch with the lady at Kintalla, and she insisted I go there for lunch. However, I'll be back to see the start of the race, and then I'll hand over the cup and go. Tell me about the school."

"Sure. But where should I start?"

"I want to know about the young genius that Joan Ker first spotted. If she hadn't put her finger on him, Michael Mackay might have been turned aside into some dead end as a wee eccentric. She gave him all she knew. And then, mercifully, you took it from there. What is the score now?"

So Raeburn told him, and also about the junior technology department. He said, "I'd better show you the computer room."

But Coulson said, "Relax. I've seen it, and it terrifies me. I'm afraid to think in a place like that. Somebody will know what's going on in my mind."

"Not to worry." Raeburn could laugh, for there was nothing going on in the world that could truly frighten this innovator in education. "Come back another time and see a whole junior class on the job—all these podgy little fingers going like lightning and working out things we never thought of."

They made their way through the workings of the school and the personalities in it, until Coulson said, "Barry, I couldn't be happier. Off soon to Kintalla, but could you make my day by letting me come to the morning service?"

"I was hoping you would say that. Starts in ten minutes. We'll walk up."

"Of course. I'm an elderly sentimental, but it is a great day for me."

In the great hall Raeburn had to forge forward to his seat at the front, leaving Coulson to slip into the farthest back seat, without fuss. The chaplain set the occasion off with a brief prayer, and the music master took over.

He made it clear that this was a time, not so much to worship God, but to rehearse for the end-of-term concert. The whole ceremony was devoted to the practice of a great hymn that seemed to have become the rousing challenge of the school. It was "Guide Me, O Thou Great Jehovah," and they roared into it with great spirit.

Outside, Raeburn and Coulson shook off gently the small

horde that clung to them, and walked to Coulson's car. The old headmaster was saying, "I'm very glad, Barry, you have kept this going. Now, I'll see you at the start of the race. And I'll give your compliments to herself." Dr. Coulson swung himself into his car and was away.

He was among the foremost of the spectators when they assembled for the start at two-thirty that afternoon. The course stewards had the flags out and the road sections checked, while on the lawn at the main gateway to the school there was a table laid with the trophy displayed, and a seat or two for the dignitaries. In the last five minutes before the start Rankine was in the throng, encouraging and mildly threatening. They were forming a straggling line, as they had seen the great athletes do on television, with their discarded track suits like molehills scattered on the grass.

Dr. Coulson, boyishly eager as ever, his white tufts of hair bristling, would not sit down, nor would the local dignitaries, and in the end somebody gave the order to take the chairs away. Rankine barked them into line (it took three lines, but somehow the likely winners had got themselves to the front) and at last he fired his starting gun, and they were away.

A trotting group forged at once to the front, electing themselves to be among the top finishers. The rest bunched back, glad to be thought worthy to compete but with no hope of challenging the likely winners. In this group Raeburn ran, not as a competitor but as an invigilator. In the long preparations for the course he had spotted the place where the road course finished and the three times round the inside course began, and where a fly man, for mischief, could drop out for a full lap and come back restored for the final lap from among the trees, and finish freshly. So he dropped out at that place and waited to make sure defaulters did not linger with him.

In due course he jogged back to the start round the trees bordering the main playing pitch, and was among the spectators at the start minutes before the first of the finishers appeared.

They came from the end of the far straight, tiny, striving creatures, three of them seeming in a line, and bobbing towards the
goal so distant that nobody at the finish line could hear their
effort. They were nearly three hundred yards away before voices
started to say, "Hughes is leading," or, "It's very close. Ander-
son is in front." And so they thumped to the end, where somebody noted their names and their brief fame as the pack
swarmed after them.

They all finished at last, and it was time for the presentation of
the trophy, which the old headmaster did with great pedantic
style, in a brief speech full of comic apology for his own age and
inadequacy. He said all the right things, handed over the cup
and also a small replica, "its wee brother," to be kept by the
winner on his sideboard, assuming he ever had one, in perpetu-
ity. All of them laughed, and there was a dribble of applause.
The spectators and the school went on their way.

Raeburn escorted Dr Coulson back to his car.

"Funny thing, Barry," Coulson was saying. "I'd never have
noticed it if it hadn't been so obvious, but there was a fellow
there taking a series of pictures most intently and appearing to
concentrate almost exclusively on young Michael Mackay. All
his actions and ways of running, especially at the small jumps.
Now, I never thought that Mackay was ever going to be a world-
beater in terms of athletic prowess—you would be a better judge
than I am—but I have to tell you it wouldn't be the first time I
have had to take notice of an overly devoted attention to some
pupil in a boys' school. Am I right to be suspicious?"

Raeburn said, "Did you speak to the fellow?"

"He spoke to me. He had heard one or two of the older boys
referring to me as 'the headmaster,' and he came up to me saying, 'I think you have heard of me—Bev Capell—' Do you know
that name?"

"I've heard it. Go on."

"The rest meant little to me. He said, 'I was working for Lord
Melfort, and I had to find out how to push on with Operation

Dalshay.' I'm pretty sure that was the name, sort of foreign, but Dalshay is as near as I can get to it—and he went on something like, 'As you know, it has to be long-term—his lordship would have put you in the picture before his accident.' I couldn't make head or tail of it, Barry. What do you think?"

"Can't say." Raeburn felt there was much here he had to ponder. "Let me think about it. If I get enlightenment, I'll give you a call."

"Okay. Don't let it bear you down. I never fancied that Melfort or anything to do with him. He hung about here a lot when the Duke was in the castle. . . . By the way, the Duchess asked me to say she would be pleased if you let her drive you to the funeral. She'll pick you up in her car in good time."

Raeburn waved Dr. Coulson down the drive, after the older man had wound down his window and said, "It's going well, Barry. The school is in great heart. Well done! See you on Tuesday."

Michael Mackay was waiting to intercept him near the entrance to the main building. He came forward with, "Sir!"

"Hullo, Michael. What's doing?"

"I was wondering, sir, if you would allow me to go to the funeral of Miss Ker. I hear there's a small party going in the school bus, and I was hoping there might be a place for me."

"I don't see why not. Have a word with Mr. Rankine and say I'd have no objection. Would you like to tell me why you are so anxious to go?"

"I don't know about funerals—I've never been to one—but Miss Ker was very good to me when I was younger. I showed her my calculations for the reserved reciprocals, and although she didn't quite understand the theory, she went over them with me and suggested ways in which I might go ahead. It was very encouraging."

"She was good at that sort of thing."

"She would always listen when I tried to explain things—I can't think of any other way I can say thanks."

"People who are dead are beyond our thanks, Mike, but we can always try to honour them. Yes, I think you should go. What's doing up in the tower?"

"Not much, sir. I'm tidying up, so that there won't be too much to be seen by the visitors, if any of them ever come. Would you like to see?"

They climbed the stairs together, the boy saying, "I've let the satellite go, for I won't need it anymore if my experiments are going to be done from some other place."

For the want of something not too technical to say, Raeburn asked, "Tell me, would you have any idea how many satellites are up there?"

"That's a good question." There was no patronising note; perhaps even a trace of admiration. "I can't say I've counted them all—I doubt anyone has. But I did a rough calculation at the time I was choosing one to ride on, and came to the conclusion there might be about two thousand active up there. Maybe even as many as two and a half thousand."

"Pretty crowded."

"Oh, there's lots of room. Here, sir, I'll show you the charts I made." The boy was pulling sheets from a drawer.

"Well, never mind. I'm sure your guess is accurate. One thing I wanted to ask you, Mike. Does the word 'Dalsay,' or something like it, mean anything to you?"

Mackay was alert. " 'Dalshay?' Where did you come across that, sir?"

"Never mind that just now. It means something to you, eh?"

"Yes. I can't think how you came to learn of it. Sorry if that sounds cheeky. Well, it's a Russian word that has been turning up recently in their signals—there seems to be a programme with that name. A submarine is building as part of the scheme, but of course it hasn't turned up yet in our waters. Probably not launched yet."

"Do you know what the word means?"

"I found it in the Russian dictionary in the library: it means something like 'distant future.' Where did you hear it?"

"Ah, well, leave it for the moment."

"If you like, I can ask the gentleman from the Admiralty. He should be here any day now."

"Don't bother. No, on the whole I don't think it is something we should be speculating on until we have a better idea of what ought to be done."

"You know best, sir."

"That's the trouble—I don't. Maybe there is no best. Enough of that, though." Raeburn was looking round the tangle of wires and apparatus. "I don't see much change, however. Would you like to tell me what you have dismantled, and what you have kept? And by the way, let me talk now as the headmaster, my advice is that you shouldn't go beyond anything you haven't already shown to me or to Mr. Baillie. You are dealing with things that may be more important than you think. Agreed?"

"I think you're right, sir. All I was planning to show was the sight table and the screen with the vision into the Atlantic. The satellite I was using has started to send out interference signals. I could deal with that, but I'd like to hear what the expert says."

"Keep in touch, Michael. Sorry I can't be more helpful. It's all a bit beyond me."

"Not to worry, sir. It's beyond most people."

8

The next day was Monday, and from the start it looked as if it was to be a Monday like any other Monday, which was exactly what it turned out to be. But all Mondays pass, and when Tuesday came there was the bustle of all the matters, welcome or not, that come to disrupt the routine. Raeburn, emerging early from his quarters, still was able to gather up a few pupils and take them, with end-of-term eagerness, for a brief jog round the grounds, although his heart was not in it. When breakfast was over, he came out again to meet the school bus and the small party that was setting off, almost too early, it seemed, to attend the funeral.

Raeburn looked over the group, which awaited his inspection but was eager to be off, for a change of routine was always welcome. The faithful Rankine, installed in the driving seat, was in charge, and Henderson, the music master, was already wearing his air of haggard authority.

Henderson dismounted from the bus and reported, "I thought we ought to have some real music for Miss Ker. I have shaped them quickly—if only there had been more time!—into what used to be called a double quartet. We have had one or two rehearsals, and we'll have a run-through once or twice in the bus. We'll go early, and I'll have a word with the minister and the organist and persuade them to let me take over the organ in the crematorium. Does that sound a bit high-handed?"

"No hand could be too high for the mission we are on." Raeburn gave him a reassuring smile. "You are a rascal, Edward, but an artist as well, which is better." He waved them away.

The arrival of the Duchess was heralded by the thumping trumpets from the huge engine of the Iglietti coupé. She sat at the wheel, her great red mass of hair lightly bound, and they greeted each other.

"Ready?" she asked.

He gestured toward the car. "Not, I should have thought, a funeral chariot."

"Never mind. She would have appreciated the style, and so do I and so do you. We'll park in a side street at Ayr and walk to the place, pausing someplace where I can do up my hair. Would you like to drive?"

"I was desperate for you to suggest it. Move over and be ready for squalls."

He edged the car carefully along the driveway and out through the gates, nodding gravely in passing to the few surprised pupils who saw them go. Once on the main road, he turned to smile at her.

"New car again?"

"Yes. Delivered to me last week. We're down to get one a year at Kintalla. The company is based in Milan. He owns more than half of it."

"No comment," said Raeburn, "except to say that it would be difficult to give a more adequate answer. Which way? The coast road?"

"Yes. I prefer it. We can come back through the hills if you like."

They rolled comfortably alongside the North Channel, through Ballantrae and Lendalfood and Girvan, talking little. At one point, guessing that his mood was right, she said, "I think I knew about you and Joan Ker. Am I right?"

"You are. What they call a one-off."

"It might have come to more than that, I think."

"It might. I think it would have."

"It deserved to. Let's talk about something that might fairly be called, in a way, my business. Have you heard anything more about the Melfort thing?"

"Not a word."

"Nor I. I'd rather have it that way."

Raeburn said, "Still, I think you ought to know. . . ." He told her about Bev Capell. "There may be nothing to be worried about, but I don't think we've seen the last of him."

She was quick to say, "Take no risks, Barry, especially at this time. I guess you are saying that anything touching Melfort hasn't got much good in it, and I agree. I think I'll ask Reid and Macfarlane to take a special interest in Markland and yourself. With no house parties at Kintalla they haven't got much to do anyway, and it will keep them out of mischief."

"I shouldn't have thought that pair were ever far away from mischief."

They laughed and changed the subject.

At Ayr they parked the car and she disappeared to put her hair in order. Walking to the crematorium, she said, "Barry, is this going to upset you badly?"

"Not badly. Not now. But I suppose she will always be somewhere in my mind."

"I'll not mention her again."

Not many people had gathered to see her into the shades. The Markland party was already in place, with the music master at the organ, whispering fiercely to the pupils grouped around him. In the front seat was Joan's married sister, a matronly figure in black, and her husband and young family. Dr. Coulson's white hair shone from a few seats back. Others might be distant relatives, and perhaps teachers from the school where Joan had been most recently.

Men in black, with features of schooled gravity, carried the coffin forward, a touchingly small box, it seemed to Raeburn.

The minister took his place and announced, "We shall commence the service with the singing of the thirtieth paraphrase, to the tune Kedron."

The Markland choir gave out the words with such resounding firmness that there was no need but to fall silent and listen, and this the tiny congregation did gladly, listening to the words which might in their youth have been familiar, but which had rusted in their thoughts through decades of indifference.

> Come, let us to the Lord our God
>   with contrite hearts return;
> Our God is gracious, nor will leave
>   the desolate to mourn.

At the end the preacher read some verses from the New Testament, said a short prayer, and announced that there was to be another hymn.

This time it was the one the Welsh love and which Raeburn and Dr. Coulson had heard the whole school rehearse. After it the preacher paused; then he proceeded to give up the body to the unseen flames.

After another pause they all stood and started to leave. Dr. Coulson put a hand on Raeburn's shoulder, saying, "I couldn't have stood much more."

"Nor I. Could you say a word to Henderson? He told me he would be sticking to Joan's favourites."

They dispersed quickly. The Duchess spoke to people here and there and then moved quietly to the street corner where Raeburn joined her. As they walked to the car, she said, "It must mean something, I hope, to be loved like that. And to be seen away with the songs that have helped you."

"It must," he said.

She said, "I'll drive now if you don't mind. And I hope you don't mind the long way home."

"Good idea. Anyway, your bodyguards told me only the other day it might be wise not to go back, at this time, the way you come. Incidentally, thanks for wanting to be there."

They did not talk much for the first hour, on the southwest part of the journey. It was a fair day, with the dappled clouds under the blue sky, and a breeze from the moors. They stopped more than once through the Lowthers to take in the view of little waters and hills where snow wreaths stayed, and where the heather that would flame at the end of summer still lay dead-looking, and white farmhouses, and rich green straths where fat herds rejoiced in idleness.

Soon they turned west out of Nithsdale, and at a copse that looked over to Tynron she pulled the car aside off the road, switched off, and said, "Food."

"What? Here?"

"Where else? I have a hamper. I'll spread a rug here on the grass, and you lift the hamper over. Don't drop it. There are breakables in there."

The breakables were the bottle of wine, in a cooler, and glasses. And sandwiches, and dishes of this and that. She spread the feast out.

He said, "I say! This is too good for me."

She looked at him steadily. "Barry, nothing is too good for you."

"When you say things like that, I get scared." They both laughed, until she said, "I believe you are safer now than you have ever been."

So they feasted, looking toward Dalmacallan Forest. The wind died, and there was more heat in the sun. They reclined where they were, while she asked questions about the school and especially about the junior technology department. He said, "You must come oftener and see what's going on. I'm not the one to give detailed explanations."

After a while, when he seemed to be musing, he changed the subject, saying, "One thing I have in my mind at this moment. . . ."

"Speak up."

"It's this. It may be an old wives' tale, but I have often heard that a funeral is an occasion that makes the average man get amorous ideas. I believe it's also said about christenings."

"What about weddings?"

"I dare say. I haven't been to many weddings. I'm bound to tell you that the funeral thing is true of me at this moment."

"It sounds like the canny start of a proposition."

"Tell me," he said, "would the same thing be true of women?"

She thought before speaking. "I can't answer for all women, but I think they tend to be more careful about the time and place."

"Offended?"

"Not in the least. Friends are for telling things to."

He kissed her then, gently, as if they were old kissing acquaintances. The touch of her cool lips stirred him strangely, evoking memories of which he had so few. She did not draw away when he repeated the kiss, but her lips smiled slightly.

Then he reached over to touch her. She did not fend him off, but met his eyes, her head shaking mildly in refusal; he took his hand away.

"Not here. Not now. Time to go." She set to gathering up the picnic things, stowing them carefully again in the hamper. They took to the road in silence.

This time the road ran southwest direct through Galloway, running into the sun that was starting his long dive into the sea. She resumed the conversation, and he was happy again. He said so.

He looked at her. She said nothing, but was nodding. So the miles passed at ease, and they were into the Rhinns of Galloway, and running down towards the Mull. She said suddenly, interrupting a train of conversation, "There can't be anything for you to do in connection with the school at this time of day. We'll go to Kintalla. Fletcher will take you home later."

Fletcher came out from his gatehouse as she stopped the Iglietti. They got out as she gave instructions. "Put the car away, please, Mungo. You can run Mr. Raeburn home later. I'll let you know when. And would you hand the hamper into the kitchen?"

"I'll do that, Your Grace."

Stretching their legs, they walked down the drive. The great house seemed empty. She made them drinks as they talked on, with certain silences where they were apt. After a time she said, "We are reaching the stage when we are not really talking; we are just saying things."

She crossed the room to him, and this time he took her fully into his arms. Her response was unmistakable. As they stepped apart, she took him by the hand, saying, "Come with me."

They went up the broad stairway. She went forward and opened a door. "Come in," she said.

He stood in her bedroom, a room faintly scented. Again she entered his embrace, staying there, until she said, "No need to hurry, dear lad. We have all the time we need."

He said, "We can give great comfort to each other."

"No two people I can think of need and deserve it more."

"I have been thinking that for a long time."

So they were not fevered in their preparations, not hurrying into the bed, but exploring and fondling with small whisperings. He would say, "I have been an infrequent performer, and never once without love."

She would reply, "Love is what you will find here."

His hands feasted hungrily upon her nakedness and were made welcome. At last she turned, saying, "Now."

The moment was blessed and timeless, to be remembered after for the perfect matching they achieved. When it was over, they lay in stillness together.

He slept then, for minutes, as men tend to do for renewal, while she lay quietly and doted on his dependence on her. Soon they were loosely embraced and talking—not of great or poetic things, but of their lives long apart. They talked of themselves, while outside the afternoon went past.

They came downstairs eventually, grateful to feel that the naturalness had not diminished. Nothing was said about the future. She rang for Fletcher, who came up the drive in the estate wagon. Raeburn moved to say some memorable words of fare-well, but, smiling, she put her hand over his mouth and kissed him behind the door.

Fletcher gestured him inside the vehicle, and they were away.

"Markland is it, Mr. Raeburn?"

"Markland it is—the call of duty. Thank you."

"Aye—that was a sad duty that was on you today."

For a moment Barry Raeburn did not pick up the allusion. His mind shrank with sudden guilt. *My God, Joan, have I forgotten you already?*

When the funeral party bus arrived at Markland in the early afternoon, Mrs. Gibson, the housekeeper, was waiting for them. She wanted to know how the affair had gone, and Mr. Rankine, holding the pupils gathered round him, gave her an outline of the ceremony, allowing the young members of the party to put in their contributions.

After a time she made them scatter to their duties, holding back only Rankine and Michael Mackay. When they were alone, she said, "Mr. Rankine, I'm sorry the headmaster is not here with you. An official gentleman has been here waiting to see Michael's work in the tower."

"That's all right, I think, Mrs. Gibson. Someone has been expected from the Admiralty to check up on some of Michael's experiments." He turned to young Mackay. "Will you look after him, Michael? Show him all he wants to see. Okay?"

Mackay assented. "I suppose so, sir."

"I don't want Michael kept late," Mrs. Gibson said. "Today has meant a great upset to his sleeping time. He should be lying down."

"It won't take long," said Mackay. "Where is he?"

Mrs. Gibson produced the new arrival from the main build-ing. He came forward with hand outstretched to Rankine, say-ing, "Hughes. Admiralty. I take it you are Raeburn, the head-master."

"Don't take it. My name is Rankine, and I am his deputy. This young man is Michael Mackay, who will look after you."

The newcomer put an arm round Mackay's shoulders, and the boy shrank away slightly. "Okay, young fellow, no time to lose. Let's go."

When Raeburn arrived at the school, where he was set down by Mungo Fletcher, Rankine was waiting for him. Raeburn listened to his story of the arrival, and said, "Better send Mackay to me. I want to hear how it finished."

Mackay told him. "I'm sorry to say, sir, I didn't like him much. I showed him the screen and the long-distance viewing, and he took a lot of notes. But there was something odd about the sort of questions he asked."

"Odd? How do you mean?"

"Well, he wanted to know if I had logs of all the foreign vessels I had identified. I'm afraid I said no. As I have told you, I have full notes, only I didn't feel I wanted him to get at this stuff."

Raeburn said, "You may be right. Anyway, as we have agreed, you have a free hand on your special experiments. Tell me, would you say he was a real boffin, well-informed?"

"Up to a point, sir, but frankly, I came to the conclusion there was something not quite genuine about him. It struck me to ask him if he had any identification on him."

"And then?"

"He was pretty angry. Called me impertinent and whatnot. I knew then I might be on the right track, and I absolutely insisted. He was in a rage, but he said eventually he had an official letter of identification in his car, and banged away to get it. That was the last I saw of him. He just got into his car and drove away."

"That's all?"

"Absolutely, sir, except that I had taken his car number. Here it is."

"You seem to have done a good job, Michael. Let's call it a

day. I guess you have been up since dawn, so what about bed now?"

"I'd be glad to. Good night, sir."

Back in his rooms, Raeburn dialled a number, until a voice said, "Aye?"

"Reid—this is Barry Raeburn."

"Mr. Raeburn? What can I do for you?"

The gamekeeper listened to the story of the Admiralty man, and then he said, "I'll write down the car number. Give me it again," and, "I can find the name of the owner almost right away. I know who to phone. I'll be ringing you again in half an hour, maybe less."

Raeburn was prepared to wait. As he settled to it, his phone rang.

A female voice at the other end said, "Mr. Raeburn? Is that the headmaster speaking?"

"It is."

"Mr. Raeburn, I have tried several times to get you on the phone today. I have a message from Mr. Geoffrey Hughes of the Admiralty. I am his secretary."

"Do go on."

"As you know, it had been arranged that Mr. Hughes would be calling at the school about this time to appraise the work of a certain pupil. Unfortunately he has not been able to hold to this arrangement, and asks if you will be good enough to defer it until after Easter. He has been called at short notice to sit in on a presummit meeting in Washington, leaving this morning. He asks me to convey the apologies of the department and himself. There is a letter in the post to you."

"I see . . . of course, after Easter would be quite all right . . . perhaps more suitable in some ways." Raeburn pondered briefly: *What the devil should I say now?* "There is no likelihood that he could have changed his plans at the last minute—and still be in this country?"

"None at all, Mr. Raeburn. I drove him to the airport this

morning, and he has since been on the phone from Washington."

"Thank you. I am most grateful. Good-bye."

The phone rang again. "It's Reid, sir. The car—it's registered in the name of the organisation called Melfort Holdings. I must say I'm not surprised to hear it."

"Well, well! There's a lot to all this." He told Reid about the false Hughes, and was answered, "There is nae doot he is one of Lord Melfort's gang. A lot here tae think aboot. I never fancied his lordship much anyway."

"And didn't you and Macfarlane prove it! By the way, it would be a good idea if you both were around the school grounds until we see the end of this."

"We'll do just that."

9

There is nothing more challenging than a new tradition. In the short time during which both schools had existed, it had become the practice that the schools' rugby teams met to celebrate the end of that year's football season. This year it was Glendochart's turn to visit Markland. A small party gathered at the main entrance to greet the visitors.

The bus swung into the drive. The Glendochart teachers came first, and when the boys started to descend, it could be seen that the arriving players were far bigger, fitter, and tougher than the Markland boys. They would be a hard lot to beat in these final games.

They walked round the grounds, inspected the pitch, while the visiting captains heeled knowingly into the turf in some sort of superstitious analysis, with the Markland players looking on, hiding their apprehensions. Raeburn at last signalled for silence.

The Glendochart headmaster announced, "Attention, please, gentlemen. The junior game to start in half an hour, so these players to change at once. There will be a twenty-minute interval between games to allow the seniors to change. Referees to be provided by Markland—Mr. Rankine for the juniors, and—need I say—Mr. Barry Raeburn to referee the seniors."

There was a dribble of cheering as the juniors ran off to get ready. The whole of Markland was now assembling round the pitch, with some of the locals arriving to cheer their home team. Raeburn went here and there among them, speaking to those he knew and, because some of them were parents, remembering to give the expected expert assessment. The chief thing that the parents wanted was reassurance and even comfort, in many cases not so much in terms of their children's scholastic ability, as of their character and vigour, how they would face the world, for which the parents often felt they had themselves done little to prepare their children. Often in these encounters Raeburn had felt that he was educating not the children but their fathers. These men were no doubt formidable in business, but never appeared so vulnerable as when, generally not even knowing the right questions to ask, they sought information about their own, whom, by handing their development to strangers, they had virtually abandoned.

At last Raeburn was able to attend to the game, with the junior teams running onto the field. As the players lined up, there were cries from the young spectators. Rankine blew his whistle, and the game started.

In a junior game of rugby the play tends to start quietly. As the ball goes about the field, the team tends to herd in a bunch after it, abandoning their instructions, constantly renewed in practice, to open out across the field and to mark their opposite number. It could be seen at once that the Markland boys were smaller and lighter than the well-fed and well-schooled creatures opposite.

As the teams lined up for the kickoff, Mackay's voice could suddenly be heard. It had an unexpected hardness of authority.

"Spread out," he was saying. "Spread out! Get your man!" And Raeburn felt himself smiling inwardly, thinking of commands that this ingenious scrap of humanity might be giving to some other team, perhaps not so far ahead.

From the kickoff, the ball somehow came back to the Markland side, and, "This way!" Mackay was demanding from his position on the school's right wing. It brought to the minds of his teammates some remembered drill, and the ball came fast along the line and into his hands. The big opposing forwards were coming upon him, some of them slowing as they expected him to kick into touch since they were not leaving him any room to run. He poised briefly and made a high measured kick down the touchline.

Most of the players waited for it to go out of play, and few of them seemed to notice that Mackay had run off the field and was sprinting down the side of the pitch and out of play. The ball overshot the opposing fullback, and as it bounced, Mackay had swerved back into the field of play and caught it on the rise. He was by this time past all the Glendochart players, although one or two of them chased him vainly as he cut inside to ground the ball below the posts. Rankine whistled and signalled a try.

"Touch," panted the breathless Glendochart captain to Rankine, the referee, who replied, "Ball never out of play," and waved them behind the line for the conversion kick. Mackay himself took it and put it over the bar neatly.

Twice again the move worked. At halftime the teams turned round with the score 16–4 in favour of Markland. One of the Glendochart masters spent half a minute of the interval talking to his puzzled team.

The second half was a desperate struggle to keep the bigger Glendochart boys out. Great cries of encouragement came now continually, and through the confusion were the commands of Mackay. At last, but only once, the Glendochart fellows battered their way over at the Markland corner but again failed with the kick. The home team came off the pitch with a 16–8 victory, the first time in history that the juniors had beaten their rivals.

The victorious team members were swept away in triumph by their seniors, who were now running to strip for their own contest. Raeburn stayed on the pitch, already in his referee kit and ready for the fray. But he went aside to where the spectators were thinly scattered. The man called Bev Capell was there, coming to meet him. All through the junior game he had prowled the touchline with his camera, photographing the running and leaping figure of Michael Mackay.

Capell was now coming forward to speak to Raeburn, and he

wore a look of ingratiating readiness. Barry Raeburn allowed him the first word.

"You are Mr. Raeburn, the headmaster," he said, as if they were old acquaintances. "I made a cock of it the first time, Mr. Raeburn. You may have heard. I started in talking to an old guy who used to be the headmaster and I thought it was you. Fortunately, I don't think he knew what the hell I was talking about, so he doesn't seem the kind of old sod who would blow the gaff. I might have known it was likely to be somebody on his toes like you. I have something to show you first."

Raeburn nodded, signalling for both of them to stroll to the shade of the trees. "Carry on," he said.

"Can anybody hear us here? Is it all right?"

"Absolutely all right. But hurry. I haven't much time. What have you got?"

Capell took from an inside pocket a pack of photographs and handed them over. Raeburn noticed the stains on his fingers, the marks of the old-fashioned photographer. He riffled quickly through the prints. They were all of Michael Mackay.

"I took these at the race the other day. Developed them in the hotel. I've got another lot from the game today. He's quite a kid."

Raeburn tried to nod wisely. "So what," he asked, "do we do now?"

The other said, "It all depends on what Lord Melfort's people say, but I have a good idea. We understand Melfort was about to put you in the picture. You know—about Dalshay. The ones who come after him—I've been in touch with them—and they told me even more than I knew before. I have to carry on, they said, but when I spoke to them this morning, they said just to cover the game today and then to report back. It looks as if I'll be seeing you again, Mr. Raeburn. You look like the kind of gentleman, if I may say so, that I could work with."

Raeburn tossed the fragments of this puzzle in his brain, finding no solution. But there might be ways of at least extending the available facts.

"Who knows," he said ponderously, "how it will work out for all of us? I have to go now. If you wait here at the end of the trees, I shall send a couple of reliable chaps to help you on your way. You can trust them."

Capell was doubtful. "Are they with us?" he asked.

"All the way." Raeburn ran from him. There were ten minutes to go before the senior game was due to start.

He found Reid and Macfarlane lurking at the wall of the dressing rooms. They had been passing a half-bottle between them, and seemed none the less alert for that.

He told them about Capell, and the mysterious significance of Dalshay, and the involvement of Melfort, and the extensive photography of Mackay and what that might mean.

"We've got to know what the whole thing is about. Can you do something, do you think?"

"Oh, well, indeed, it's very likely we can, sir."

"Aye, to be sure, Mr. Raeburn."

"Where did you say he was? At the end of the trees? With a camera?"

"We'll maybe have something to report to you later like." The two went off in the direction of Capell.

Before the senior game had even started, Reid and Macfarlane had found Capell where he had been told to wait.

"I'm Reid and he's Macfarlane. And you'll be Mr. Capell."

"Right first time, gents. Always a pleasure to deal with gentlemen. You will be the ones Mr. Raeburn told me to expect. Suppose we go to the pub down the road and have a noggin or two and talk about things of mutual interest."

"That's an awful nice idea. Noggins, indeed! There's a fine word for it." The two laughed unrestrainedly, and Capell joined in.

"We have a car just here, Mr. Capell. We'll go in that, and after we can run you back to pick up your own."

They ushered him into the back seat of the estate wagon and suddenly crowded in beside him, one on each side. He stared at each in turn.

"You fellows," he said, "are right comics."

"Like enough. We have our own ways of doing things here."

Only a moment passed before Capell found his hands and his legs bound. A strip of wide sticky tape found its way across his mouth, and he was down on the floor of the car, with Macfarlane gripping him. Reid emerged and took the driver's seat, setting off through the side roads towards the moors. In the back, Macfarlane had his hands on one of Capell's ankles. Several times the captive heaved in an effort to be upright; each time a hard thumb plunged deep into a nerve end, bringing a bubbling moan from the trussed-up figure, who at last lay still and submissive.

The car emerged from the valley floor and was climbing to the high moorland, where they left the road and took a track alongside a river bursting from hill lochs and boggy moors. At one point Reid got out and unpadlocked a gate, put there to discourage the curious hill walker, since it was decorated on the high side with razored barbed wire. Beyond, the track lessened to hard wheel marks, until they were on turf rarely visited.

They came to rest at a high bank where a waterfall foamed from a rocky plateau. Here they dragged Capell out to a small hidden patch of grass ringed by a brake of low juniper bushes. He was moaning behind his gag as they unlocked his shackles and pegged him out on his back, arms and legs spread-eagled. The two men took their jackets off and laid them tidily aside.

Macfarlane bent down and ripped off the gag.

"What the hell is this about, you bastards! This will be the worst day you've ever lived. Let me up, damn you—now!"

"Ach, it'll be a good while afore ye're up oot o' there."

Capell struggled and at last collapsed back, starting to yell. At last he realised his cries for help were useless, and fell silent.

"That's a wee bit better, now. Anyway, what with the waterfall noise and with nobody aboot, you haven't a chance of anybody hearing you."

"For Christ's sake, what are you going to do to me?"

"Well, to be sure, we're just going to listen to you."

They turned aside to the car, gathering up some tools. At their backs, on the edge of the grassy precipice overlooking the waterfall, there was an ancient cairn, an old monument to a Covenanting zealot who had run to this place from his enemies and had been shot down. His martyrdom was brief, and its preliminaries less painful than the fate of his wife, who long outlived him, with her thumbs crushed and flattened by the screws they had used on her, in vain, to make her tell them where they could find her husband. But her cries had brought him near the house, and they had pursued and killed him. So it was an apt place for cruelty.

"You see," Reid was saying, "you know a few things that some of us would like to hear aboot. There is plenty of time, but you would be wise to talk as fast as you can." He was absently snipping the air with a pair of steel wire cutters.

"I don't know anything. I swear by God . . ."

"You don't need to swear. It would be easier if you told us right away. Easier for yoursel'. Like aboot Dalshay and what that might mean, and where the lad Mackay comes in, and what the pictures are for, and who you tell all this to, just the way you are going to tell us, and all that sort of thing."

The other said, "Of course, there will be many another thing. We wouldn't know, but for sure you do. And ye'll tell us, and we'll be all the wiser."

"Aye, and another thing. What aboot Lord Melfort? His lordship is a clever one, and he must have had a great hand in all this. I think it's time we started, Mr. Capell. I'm sure you won't disappoint us—"

"—or keep us waiting too long."

They started by kneeling close to him and asking the questions. Being hill men, they had voices used to carrying over valleys, easily piercing the uproar of the waterfall. Capell's deni-als turned into a screaming squeak, but these continued for long, as if he had much to hide and protect. So, with seeming reluc-tance, they started to work on him.

Some of the answers came in time, with the steel cutters stain-ing as they were plied from the fingertips inward in small lengths. His martyrdom lasted far longer than Hugh MacCul-loch's, the name written on the memorial cairn, and it was inevi-table that long after he had told all that he had to tell, they kept on, so that in the end he was clearly inventing, and they realised that he was finished. As they rose to their feet, nodding in satis-faction, he was limp and silent. It had not been necessary to stifle his long lamentations. That had been the task of the waterfall. His hands, still spread in his bonds, were now no more than palms, where the reddening stumps showed what had been done.

Raeburn sat late in his room, after dark, with the satisfaction of a day well spent. He was remembering what he had said to the few parents who had been present, and had checked up on some of their son's records, taking notes so as to be able to remember them the next time round, for many of them would be at the end-of-term concert.

There was also much in his mind: the events since the death of Melfort, killed on their own admission by these hard men Reid and Macfarlane, who had told him that Melfort had to go before they—who are "they"?—would wipe him out, Raeburn himself. He had no sorrow for Melfort, but there was a growing appre-hension at the menace to the whole life of the school, somehow vulnerable now for reasons mysterious. He made some notes in an attempt to clear his mind, but the words did not help.

It seemed to him that there was a gentle tap at the window. He sat listening for a time, and after moments there was another, from a hand that might be demanding entry. He braced himself to lift the heavy curtain aside. Two figures stood there, dimly outlined. As he bent forward to see them more clearly, the nearer one, who was Reid, touched a hand to his cap, and immediately put a finger to his lips. Macfarlane was stolid in the background, unrecognisable.

Raeburn, in silence, gestured for them to go round to the front door. Reid shook his head, motioning to the window. Raeburn heaved up the heavy sash, holding the curtain aside. Both men climbed into the room. Macfarlane eased the window down and pulled the curtain across it. They stood on his carpet, taking their caps off courteously.

"We got some information for you, sir," said Reid.

Macfarlane added, "It might not keep. We thought you would be the better for hearing it right away."

Raeburn greeted them and put them into chairs. "Fine! But at this time of night, it's better if we all start with a good dram. Any objections?"

"Night or day," said one of them, "there never is a bad time to have a dram."

"Indeed, and that's a fine drop, Mr. Raeburn. From Speyside, I would say."

"You would be right," Raeburn told them, naming the malt distillery. "Drink up. An old friend owns the still and sends me a case every wee while. Have you had a busy day yourselves?"

Reid looked long into his glass, absently allowing Raeburn to pour another. "A case of that would be riches indeed." He drank. "Aye, sir, indeed and we have been busy. There's a lot to tell you."

Macfarland added, "It took a long time to get the story out of him. But we managed. Aye, we managed."

Reid laid his glass down and was speaking. "This Dalshay thing is a Russian project to go beyond the stars on a space voyage that will last for the best part of a lifetime—forty to fifty years at least. They are building the machines now, hoping to set off in less than two years. It can only be done if they get a crew of very young people who are clever enough. They've looked everywhere, and the only inside one they can get is a clever wee lassie of twelve from Latvia. She has their scientists guessing, and she is busy learning new tricks. They need one more crew at least, and that's where young Mackay comes in. They've been sizing him up for the job."

Raeburn blew, saying at last, "But—but—well, if this is true, it explains a lot of things. But what if Mackay, or his people, refused to go?"

It was Macfarlane who answered. "No problem. They were meaning to lift him."

"Kidnap him—from here?"

"Just that. He would have got the treatment and get taught the language and some of the new scientific things."

"Go on. What about all these photographs? What's the point of them?"

"He told us they would have to find out about Mackay in every way—how he walks and stands and runs and balances—all that. It's a bit beyond us, but that is what he said."

"And Melfort—what about him? Where did he come in?"

"His lordship was their agent. He was the key man here and in other countries, and was in good favour because he claimed to have discovered the Mackay boy. I tell you, sir, we are well rid of that gentleman."

Raeburn, knowing he would not readily get his head cleared this night, poured them another dram. "This man Capell—he seems to have been very cooperative. How did you manage that?"

"Do you think he told us all you wanted to know?"

Raeburn asked, "Are you sure you got the right man? You would know Capell by the stains on his fingers from photographic chemicals."

The two men studied each other, as if deciding who should answer. Then they chuckled, and Reid said, "Ach, you know sir, he didn't have much in the way of fingers by the time his story was finished."

Raeburn, guessing wildly and then putting the answer aside, said, "Where is he now, then?"

"You needn't worry about him, for it's not very likely he will come back down from the moor. There are pools in these bogs that have no bottom to them. He's the sort of chap that could fall in."

"Oh, for God's sake, don't tell me any more. I don't want to know what the hell you have been up to."

"We've been protecting you, sir, the way the Duke ordered. He knows you are not the sort that would go about talking."

"Wait a minute, though. The car—he had a car."

Macfarlane finished his drink and let the glass hang poised. He said, "Aye, indeed—there was a car, right enough. But you know, this is a dangerous coast, and there is a place at the roadside just not very far from here where a car might drive over the cliff and fall into the sea."

They sat for a while with their drinks. Raeburn said, "So you've got it all settled?"

"So far, sir. Only so far. You never know what's next. But you may be sure we'll not be far away."

There was another pause, and both men stood up at the same time. "Time to go."

They parted the curtains and were lifting the window when Raeburn said, "How about the front door this time?"

"Not for us, Mr. Raeburn. We're not ones for doing things that's usual. Good night, sir."

The last that Raeburn saw of them were their heavy boots disappearing over the windowsill. Once outside, they lowered the window quietly and were away. A long time later, Raeburn went to bed.

10

Raeburn had finished with his correspondence by the early morning of the next day and was turning to the day's timetables when Jo Anne came back into the office.

"I'm sorry, headmaster, an unexpected parent outside, and he looks ready to be pretty angry."

"Okay, Jo Anne. We'll see him at once. What name?"

"Dr. Allen, father of Frances Allen."

"Can't think of any trouble there. Her class work is pretty good—above average—and she is ahead of the rest in her essay writing. Get out her file and show him in."

Dr. Allen came bursting into the room, a tall, broad man with a red face, who strode over to Raeburn's desk, ignoring the outstretched hand.

"Yes, I know you bloody well, Raeburn. I've seen you before, plenty of times. Can you think of any reason why I don't break your bloody neck?"

He flung a large thin book onto the desk, and shouted, "You have a lot to answer for, you bastard, and I'm here to listen to what the answer is. After that you will be bloody lucky if you don't get a few years in jail."

Raeburn, still seated at his desk, gestured the big man to a seat; after a time, Allen subsided, his threats turning to mutterings and then silence.

"Well now," said Raeburn, "believe me, I have not the faintest clue about what is happening. Perhaps it would be useful for both of us if you could tell me what this is about. I should be grateful if you found it possible not to make a scene and to keep your voice down. In this school we try to reduce hysteria to the minimum."

"That's the trouble with you cool bastards—you always think you can talk yourselves out of trouble. It won't work. There's enough here"—he pointed to the book—"to get you a stretch."

Raeburn said, "It occurs to me that you have said enough to make for a good slander suit. However, one thing at a time." He lifted the book. "Tell me what this is—Exhibit A?"

Allen gritted his teeth, trying to master his rage. "There is enough here to get you hounded out of this school."

"Well, tell me about it."

The other man leaned across the desk, pounding the book. "I gave this book to my daughter at Christmas. It's a diary. She has no mother, you know."

"Of course I knew you were a widower; it's my job to know such things. Frances is doing very well, though, I should say. . . . So it's a diary, and you have been reading it?"

Allen gulped, clasping his trembling hands on the desk. His anger was just and precious to him, and he would not let it go. He said, "She came home for the weekend last Saturday and forgot to take the book away when she left on Sunday night. I found it lying about. If I tell you it is private—intimate—I expect you know what it is about."

"Not a clue."

"It's about you. Now do you know what I mean?"

"Still not a clue."

"As I have said, you are a liar and a successful one, but not this time. Read the diary. I have marked a number of typical extracts. Go on. I'll wait."

Raeburn settled to the reading. He emerged at last with his face anxious, saying, "This is pretty unhealthy—and of course, it is pure fantasy. Not a word of truth in it. No—don't interrupt! Wait a moment." He lifted his phone.

"Jo Anne, get me Pamela Wilson—as quickly as possible." He said aside to Allen, "Wise woman, this. She'll have ideas."

Allen was holding firmly to his rage. "I can't," he said, "think of any ideas that will get you out of the trouble you are in."

They sat silently until the arrival of Miss Wilson. When she came in, Raeburn introduced the two, and she sat composedly.

"Pamela," Raeburn began, "Dr. Allen is the father of Frances Allen—"

"Oh, yes—of course I know Frances."

"He has shown me a personal diary that Frances has been keeping. Here it is. I'd like you to read the marked passages and then let us have your views on them."

She took the book, reading intently. At last she closed it, looked from one man to the other, and laughed loudly with her head back. Allen drew back, shocked. Raeburn was astounded, for he could never remember seeing her laugh before.

"So," was Allen's loud reponse, "you think that what's happened to this young girl is funny?"

Miss Wilson looked at him seriously. "Dr. Allen is it? Doctor? Medical? Is that right?"

"Yes."

"You can't be much of a doctor. This stuff is absolutely phoney."

"I might have known you people would try to stick together and brazen it out. I have reason to believe that every word of what she has written is true. She has never told me a lie. It's only too true—oh, Christ!"

Miss Wilson said, "I'm sorry for you. Here, I'm going to read you something." She opened the book at the first marked passage, saying, "Here is the entry marked the twenty-sixth of January this year:"

I must write this down before I forget every wonderful moment of it, for this was surely my day of destiny. There was a concert in the hall, given by the Strasbourg String Quartet, and everybody seemed to be carried away by the beautiful, romantic music. I was one of the last to leave the hall, for I had to close the organ for Mr. Henderson, and when I came out, who was waiting for me but darling Barry. He took my by the arm and whispered, 'Dearest Frances, would you like to come with me?' No one saw us. He led me into the bushes and suddenly embraced me passionately. Very gently he stripped me of my clothes, and then undressed. He was so beautiful. He laid me down softly on the cool grass and came down beside me, and I gave myself to him. It was the most glorious experience I have ever had. The full moon shone down on us from above, as if to bless our union.

She turned the pages briskly and announced, "Now here's the entry for February seventeenth. Mustn't miss this."

I think I ought to describe darling Barry's body to my dear diary. Of course he is a real and virile man. I am the only woman who knows every inch of him. His bottom is perfectly beautiful. Modesty forbids me to mention the more intimate parts, but what excites me almost as much is the thick mat of hair on his chest, the sign of a great athlete. It is dark and full of curls. I love to sink my hands into it and feel his lovely soft skin below.

Miss Wilson riffled busily farther into the book, paused for a moment, and said, "We'll take the last one the good doctor has marked—a fairly recent entry, dated March fourteenth:

Oh, what sweet and marvellous news! I am pregnant. Am I not the most fortunate of women? I am to bear Barry's child, and the realisation has made me deliriously happy. Just at the moment I shall not tell him, but I know that when he learns of it he will be as happy as I am. Now at last I am safe from the world and even safe from school and my old home. The baby will help to bind us together even more closely. . . .

". . . and so on. I think that will do. Unless you would like me to read the other passages Dr. Allen has marked. There is a description how Barry used to pose her naked for photography on the old sundial on the upper lawn, or how—"

"Enough, enough!" Allen burst in. "Christ, you seem to be enjoying this!"

Miss Wilson said, "I don't think I'm exactly enjoying it, but some of it is really very funny. If only for the reason that you have not recognised it for the nonsense it is."

"Prove it! By God, prove it!"

"In the first place," Miss Wilson said, "as to the concert by the Strasbourg String Quartet—when we came out of the hall at the end of the concert, there had been a heavy fall of snow. We had to get a party to dig a way out so that the players could be driven to their hotel. You can easily check that from the meteorological people. It would be easier to verify the fact that there was no full moon that night. I suppose, Doctor, that like most men, you carry about with you a small pocket diary. If you will look it up, you will see that the full moon was not until two weeks later. Go on, check."

Raeburn made no move, but Allen, like an embarrassed schoolboy, brought out his own small engagement diary and thumbed to the right page. After a time he said, "Seems to be right. No full moon any time around that date."

Then Miss Wilson said, "Next, then. We have no swimming pool in this school—although we might find a donor someday to give us one. So that we have few, if any, opportunities to examine nature's endowments. However, some months ago the headmaster and I were delegates at a conference at the Gleneagles Hotel on fitness and sports training. In our spare time we did some swimming in the hotel pool, and I was able as a dispassionate observer to notice that Mr. Raeburn is not, as it happens, endowed with a thick mat of dark curly hair on his chest. On the contrary, Dr. Allen, he has almost no hair on his chest at all, and what he has is quite white, or perhaps it would be more accurate to say off-white. In this case the proof is very easy to ascertain. No doubt Mr. Raeburn would be willing to pull up his shirt."

"Jesus Christ, go on!" Allen groaned.

"Ah, now, of course, the pregnancy. A nice touch. It happens that I have been seeing Frances every day for a time, treating her for a minor hamstring trouble. I have a diploma in physiotherapy. At the same time I attended to some small trouble she has been having with her period, about which she has seemingly never had any instruction. Nothing at all serious, but sometimes worrying to the young. We had a session only this morning. I need not go into details, but I can assure all concerned that, quite definitely, what Frances is not is pregnant. Gentlemen, I think that's the lot. I'd say that apologies are in order."

There was a silence, which Raeburn broke with the first words he had spoken since Miss Wilson had started on her dissertation. "Never mind apologies. I think it's a case of relief all round."

Allen had plunged his head into his spread hands, and they waited for him to emerge. He came up, his face haggard.

"My God! I don't know what to say. I don't know. I accept what you say. It's been hell—a nightmare. I feel as if I had come out of jail."

Raeburn said, "I should have worked it out for myself. We owe a great deal to Pamela here."

"Never mind about me," said Miss Wilson. "We have to think about Frances."

Allen paused for a long moment before speaking. "I apologize. I should not have rushed to conclusions. But my daughter's actions are unforgivable. She must have the most severe punishment."

Raeburn said, "Such as?"

"Eh, well, that's your department. . . ."

"We don't have severe punishments here, of the old-fashioned sort you probably have in mind. Give us your suggestions."

"You are pushing me, dammit. I always understood you would be responsible for discipline."

"Does that mean you agree to let us handle it in our own way?"

"Well, anyway, it's beside the point. I'll have to take her away from here."

"Why?" asked Miss Wilson.

"Good God—isn't it obvious?" Allen thumped the diary. "I couldn't expect anybody here to live with that stuff."

"Can *you?*" She was leaning forward, putting pressure on him.

"Oh, heavens, I don't know. I'll have to think out what to do. It's shattering."

She thrust the question to him: "Have you given any thought to the possibility that you could be responsible for her behaviour?"

"Me! Responsible?"

"It looks to me like a case of loneliness arising out of neglect at home. Tell me, I am sure you are a busy man professionally, but what hobbies have you? What do you do in your spare time? How do you relax?"

"What's this? The Inquisition?"

"Please answer."

"I don't know that it is any of your business, but I fish a lot, play golf, walk the hills with a camera. I get outside as often as possible."

Miss Wilson pursued it. "When did you last take Frances fishing? Or playing golf? Or even for a day on the hills?"

"But, well, her mother used to come with me. I suppose I have become a bit of a loner—anyway, Frances is only a child."

Pamela Wilson lifted the diary and shook it gently at him. "Was it a child who wrote this? Man, but you are blind. She is more than half a woman."

"A diseased mind. Horrible!"

"Nonsense. But the mind of a solitary. Your fault." She turned to Raeburn. "Do you mind if I continue this dialogue?"

"Not at all," said Raeburn. "It seems most promising."

Miss Wilson addressed them both. "You see," she said, "I recognise aspects of this that are very positive, and these we should go for. Isn't it the case, headmaster, that Frances is a writer?"

"Quite out of the ordinary," Raeburn agreed. "I take the seniors for English, and she is outstanding. She had a short story in the Christmas issue of *The Marklander* that won the first prize in the national schools magazine competition."

"But what's it got to do with—"

"Simply this, Doctor. There is an inexhaustible market for people who can write stories. We can steer her towards an interest in good writing, but you will have to play your part and be a father companion. Like all girls of that age she wants someone to love, to look up to. We have to get her off the Raeburn hook. Here's a thought. Why don't you run a dance for her during the Easter holidays? You have plenty of time to make the arrangements, and among your doctor friends there must be lots of good-looking young sons about her age or, better, just a little older."

Allen looked vaguely to both of them in turn. He said, "Do you think that would do any good? I never thought of anything like that. She seemed so young. I thought it was best to leave that sort of thing to people like you." He was lost in the human predicament—the expert looking for expert assurance from strangers.

Raeburn said, "Seems like a good idea to me. It would at least show that you have an interest. Pamela, tell us what you will be saying to her. By the way, I myself shouldn't be in on the first interview. Just you and her father. Agreed?"

"I was going to say that. We'll get her in here, Dr. Allen and I, and you will simply go and put your perfectly beautiful bottom on some other chair. Your presence would be overwhelmingly embarrassing to Frances. In fact, it would be better in the long run if she never found out that you had read the diary."

"I think that's right," he said, "if there is a right way to do it. How would you want to go about it, Pamela?"

She answered, "I'll have to play it as it comes. The first five minutes will be damnable, but we'll try to work through it. What is important is that I must be the only one to speak. You hear me, Dr. Allen? You will not say a word until I bring you in. Understood?"

Allen sat silent, his head bowed, and the other two went on with the planning.

"Tell us, though, Pamela," Raeburn insisted, "what will you be saying to her?"

She waited a long time, saying at last, "I'll have to start by telling her that her father came across her diary, which she had carelessly left about, and how distressed he was in case it might be true. Which nobody believes it was. Also she must understand how dreadfully embarrassed Mr. Raeburn would be if he knew, and how it might be ruinous to him. Then I think we sweep that aside as a juvenile indiscretion, and I go on to tell her something about the normal future for young people—the finding some other person to love and share with, the home, the family, the children. Sorry, I can't put it better than that at the moment."

Raeburn allowed Allen a pause, which he did not try to fill. So he went on, as the headmaster in judgement.

"That's fine, then, so far as we can take it. Let me sum up the position as we see it. I'll get Frances sent for. Tough as it is, we have to get to that stage as quickly as possible. I think the idea of the dance is brilliant—Allen, you must go ahead with that. I'd add this one for you, Pamela. Without reference to the diary, instruct her for me to use her Easter holiday time to outline a book-length story that would make a novel. I think it's in her. She'll bring that back to us, and if it's good enough we'll get her to finish the whole book by the end of the year. If it seems good we'll look around for some publisher who might be interested. I know a few people who might help."

"Do you—" This was from Allen. "Do you really think she could do that?"

"Why not? Here's something for you to do, Allen, as an immediate bit of action. I think we can spare Frances this evening. You go off somewhere and arrange dinner for the two of you at some expensive hotel in the neighbourhood. During that time you will not say a word about the diary. Instead, you will tell her you have arranged a week's fishing in the Easter holidays. Just you two. You have time today to go somewhere and buy her a fishing rod and all the necessary gear. Will you do that, Allen?"

"I'd be glad to."

Raeburn went on. "And don't, the two of you, take more than a few moments to get this diary thing out of the way. Everybody, young and old, has fantasies. Mostly quite harmless and never guessed at. The big indiscretion is putting them down in writing, where they might be seen by prying eyes."

Allen, much restored, groaned at this, but managed a rueful smile. Raeburn continued. "So, Dr. Allen, you have a long and useful day ahead of you. I can arrange for you to stay in the headmaster's house overnight. You can leave as early as you like in the morning. I think that's everything. Anything to add? Okay, then. I'll have Frances sent in. For God's sake, don't make too heavy weather of it."

It was late that night when Mrs. Gibson showed Dr. Allen into the lounge of the headmaster's house, where Raeburn was waiting for him. He had two glasses of whisky ready, and handed one to the doctor before saying, "Well?"

The other man sat down and toasted Raeburn before he was ready to talk.

"What a wonderful day this has been. I haven't felt like this since goodness knows when. You know, Frances seems quite grown-up. And we never mentioned the bloody diary once. Even at the first awful interview she quickly became cool. But at dinner she had all sorts of things to say. Witty things I'd never have expected. Let me tell you . . ."

Raeburn listened while Allen rambled through the details of this day with his daughter. At last he tailed off, saying, "I'm talking too much—thanks to you. Yes, a million thanks to you."

He was silent for a while, then said, "That Wilson woman. Remarkable. Very able. Tell me about her."

Raeburn told him what was necessary to establish the background and style of Pamela Wilson: the athletic renown, the dedication to the school and the pupils, the sterile tryst with the young soldier who would never get any older, the need in the school for such a bulwark.

Allen said, "I might have known. Well, I'm grateful to have seen her in action."

11

They met together at breakfast in the headmaster's lodging where Allen had slept and Raeburn had joined him from his rooms across campus.

They did not speak much over the morning meal. Allen was busy with his newspaper and Raeburn had his letters in front of him and was reading and sorting them. The last thing in their minds was any reference to the matters they had worried over in the night before.

Catching the other's eye, Raeburn pushed over to him an opened letter he had been studying, saying, "Can you be bothered? This is your field. Would you care to give me an opinion?"

It was a letter from the Medical Committee of the regional district where Markland was situated, and it intimated in formal terms that, in view of the incidence of hay fever in the area, the decision had been made that certain samples of the residents would be subjected to injections of a substance that would, as tests had proven, ensure their immunity. Markland School had been chosen as one of the test sections, since the students were healthy, and, in any case, the inoculations were harmless with no side effects whatsoever. The official letter went on to say that the medical officer, Dr. Robert Devlin, would call shortly, and the Committee would be happy to have the headmaster's cooperation.

"There's always an awful lot of stuff like this coming in from one mob or another," said Raeburn. "Either from some bureaucrat or, worse, some crank. It's a task to sort them out. This kind of thing I'd give at once to my resident medical chap, Whitfield, but I let him go away early for the Tweed fishing. What do you make of it? Do you feel like giving me some professional advice?"

Dr. Allen read the letter, then handed it back to Raeburn.

"We're a cautious lot, we doctors. It's a pity your own medical man is not here."

"Trouble?"

"I don't know. But I'm bound to say I have reservations about an experiment—that is what it is—on such a scale."

Raeburn said, "Tell me about your reservations. I had a call this morning from this Dr. Devlin, saying he'd like to call today about midafternoon, and hoping it would be suitable to muster the school in parties for the shots."

Allen hesitated. "I don't want you to think that I can't be objective about this, but I can't help thinking that my daughter would be one of these guinea pigs. You see, I don't know, and I suppose you don't know, how many of the pupils here maybe allergic to this kind of inoculation. That sort of thing will be part of the medical records."

"That settles it," said Raeburn. "I'll recall Whitfield at once."

"How long will that take?"

"He could be here in two hours at the most."

Raeburn went off to make the call. When he came back, he said, "Whitfield says there is something wrong with the arrangements—it's not in line with usual medical formalities. Would you agree?"

"I would. I haven't had much to do with institutional medicine, but he would certainly want to be here if somebody is treating his patients."

"I say—can you stay until he comes?"

"Glad to. I was only going to knock about the district doing the odd bit of fishing until I take Frances away at end of term."

"Stay here then. We have a couple of the estate gamekeepers who will get you fishing the like of which you've never seen."

"Kind of you. I'll do that."

Raeburn summoned one of the senior boys to show Dr. Allen round the school. When Dr. Whitfield arrived, still tweedy from his fish hunting, he cut short Raeburn's apologies with, "Not to worry. There wasn't a tail in the river. I'd want to be here anyway."

The two doctors quickly came to an understanding, losing themselves for a time amid an exchange of jargon and the mysteries, from which Raeburn retreated. When they emerged from this ritual, they were almost apologetic and tried to bring Raeburn into the conversation. It became clear that the two of them had been rugby players at club and university level. As both of them might be guessed at edging fifty years old, they had been giving up playing about the time that Raeburn was breaking into the big time. Raeburn could remember neither of them, but they were claiming to have played against him, and of course they went on to remember the great moments of his career that were almost too well-known, and from which it seems he was never likely to escape.

"Well," he said at last, smiling at them, "the game's over. What about having a look at our current problem?"

"That's what we're here for," Allen agreed briskly.

"Good! For a start, does anybody know anything about this Devlin?"

Whitfield left the room, saying, "Back in a minute. My office." He returned waving a red-bound volume, and explained, "Sort of directory we have. The dirt on doctors." He studied it, saying, "Not a sign of him in here. Might mean anything."

"Suspicious, for a start," said Allen. "Why don't we phone the regional health office and check up on this fellow?"

Raeburn said, "Before we do that, I think I ought to give you some inside information."

He told them about the appearance at the school of Melfort (whom he did not name), nor did he mention the last hours of the photographer, but told of his concentration upon young Mackay. He gave fuller details of the dubious Hughes who claimed to be from the Admiralty, and how he had taken off when he could produce no credentials. Even as he told it, censored, there came upon him the realisation that something was afoot that could easily be beyond any powers that he or any of his allies might have.

"You see," he said, "I suppose it would be easy to call in the police, or even the defence departments. But it would all become public then, and it would go on for months. The school would be ruined—finished—it would never recover. The publicity, trials in the courts, leaks—I don't even feel safe in bringing in the local health authority. They would insist on making it a police matter, and I'm not sure that I'd blame them."

"So what, then?" Allen asked. "And don't mistake me. Admittedly I have a daughter here, but I feel as committed to the future of the school as you do."

"My instinct is to see how far we can handle this ourselves," Raeburn said. "Should I feel guilty about that?"

"I'm with you," said Whitfield.

Allen paused briefly, then said, "Me too. We ought to know some more before we're finished with this Dr. Devlin. I hope he will feel able to be helpful."

"Better for him, perhaps. We'll go up to the headmaster's house and receive him there. Useful place. It's out of bounds and at the end of a drive, so we'll not be disturbed. We'll just hole up there and relax and wait for our visitor."

On the way, they picked up Reid and Macfarlane, who were hovering not far away. Raeburn described their roles in the operations of the Kintalla estate, and told them they had the duty for the next day or two to find good fishing for the two doctors. The four of them talked enthusiastically about the prospect.

At the house, Raeburn installed the two guests, and led the gamekeepers to a comfortable room next to the kitchen. He showed them the comforts that were available in a cupboard, which he unlocked, and described briefly the mission on which the visitor had been dispatched.

"Ach well, Mr. Raeburn," Macfarlane said, "I can see you have your doubts about that gentleman. Right enough—who can you trust nowadays?"

"Who indeed!" was Reid's contribution. "Depend on us to do the needful for you, sir, whatever that may be."

Jo Anne's car came up the drive, and a man got out with her. He was carrying a large, unusual black leather case. She showed him into the room.

"This is Dr. Devlin from the department, headmaster. You were expecting him."

After the introductions Raeburn escorted Jo Anne to the door.

"Thanks, Jo Anne. I think I'll not need you anymore for to-day. You can take the rest of the day off if you like."

He went back to the room to find the three doctors engaged in medical talk. Devlin said brightly, "I've just been making the acquaintance of my colleagues here. I didn't know there was to be a medical reception. Quite a convention, indeed."

"All doctors together," Whitfield said agreeably.

Allen cut in, "Some more than others." There was an edge to his voice, and Raeburn caught his eye, letting him see the faintest sign of a warning frown. Allen gave an imperceptible nod.

Devlin's bright voice had not changed, and he said, "We have, of course, always got to be sorting out the many quacks who invade our profession. We're pretty good at protecting our few privileges." He looked from one to the other of them. It occurred to Raeburn that it might be best to confine the discussion to the other three and to take little part himself. If this Devlin was a fraud, he was most likely to be the sort of glib fellow long accustomed to talk himself out of trouble.

Whitfield changed the subject. "Devlin," he said, "Let's hear more about this treatment."

Devlin raised a hand. "It's really quite simple," he said, pronouncing a long and authentic-sounding medical term. "Of course you will probably not have heard of it, and they'll be sure to market it under a handier name. The worthwhile thing is that there are absolutely no side effects—it goes gently even with patients who are violently allergy prone.

"The Japanese product has been tested for five years without a failure and, of course, without the results becoming known so that the newspapers couldn't hear and raise people's hopes prematurely. We've been given one of the limited samples through the E.E.C. health committee on a trial run. Of course, this school is ideal as a test. It consists of a good young mixed population, and, as is well-known"—Devlin nodded in the direction of Dr. Whitfield—"a well-organised health programme."

Whitfield mused, "There's a funny thing, now. I'm an associate member of the group practitioners' subcommittee of the E.E.C. Health Committee, and I read every word of the minutes, and there has never been a mention of this stuff."

Devlin cut in quickly, "You have to remember, it's early days." He said aside to Raeburn, "We're a pretty secretive bunch."

"Also I might have thought there would have been some sort of mention in the B.M.J.," Allen said. "They're usually fast onto a good thing."

Raeburn said, "What's B.M.J.? Isn't it some sort of magazine —a journal, isn't it? Your trade organ?"

Devlin's laugh was slightly strained. "Right first time," he said. "Good old *British Medical Journal.* Always behind the times. You can safely look for them to get onto this one in about five years." He turned from them and opened the black case. In padded nests there stood tiny phials of clear liquid, about a dozen of them, with what looked like sterile packs holding an equal number of syringes.

"There you are, gentlemen. Of course, this is only a sample pack. I have a large case in the car."

The two doctors glanced at the contents, then looked intently at the owner.

"Tell me, Devlin," said Whitfield at last, "where did you qualify?"

The man paused, then answered, "University of Edinburgh. Same as yourselves, I suppose."

"I'm Glasgow," said Allen. "That, by the way, of course."

Devlin said eagerly, "Fine faculty there. Among the very best."

Whitfield was saying quietly, "How do you account for the fact that your name does not appear in the Edinburgh list?"

Devlin looked from one to the other, not attempting to answer. A thin forced smile emerged slowly among the lines that had gathered around his mouth. The two doctors were men long accustomed to read signs that were unconcealable, and they had this fellow on the run. Raeburn watched, fascinated, under the spell of the pitiless diagnosis.

The response came at last. "Ah well, I'd better come clean. My reply was perhaps a bit simplified. The fact is, you might say that I sort of qualified here and there. I started at Edinburgh, then I spent the best part of two years at Heidelberg. Does that answer the question?"

Allen nodded. "Heidelberg? Now that's a great place for medicine. You would have, of course, come across old Professor Eichendorf, who is the top man in the field of anatomy."

"Dear old Professor Eichendorf!" Devlin was enthusiastic. "He taught me all I know about anatomy. A good man—a great teacher."

Allen sighed. "Yes, certainly—most distinguished. Except that for the last thirty years he has been the Professor of Anatomy at Madrid."

There was more fear than anger now on the man's face. He waited for a moment, then slammed the lid of his case shut, closing the clasps with shaking hands.

He stood up. "I'm getting out of here. To hell with you all— these bloody trick questions. I'm here to do an official job, and all you do is try to stop me. There will be trouble. . . ."

Raeburn stirred. "That's true—so there will." He pressed a bell push on the wall. "Devlin, you are, of course, a liar and a fraud—and probably much worse. We can easily find out if your vist here is genuine, but it would be much simpler if you were to tell us of your own free will. For instance, what is your real errand, and who sent you. That would be useful for a start."

"I am a doctor," he was shouting. "My work is confidential. You'll get nothing out of me."

Raeburn spoke to the other two. "Here's a thought. This man tells us that the serum is harmless. There's a good way to find out. He'll take a shot himself—here and now."

"Good idea!" Allen's expert hands were already in the case, and he was filling a syringe with professional detachment; while there was coming from Devlin a guttural, "No!"

"Of course, Barry," said Whitfield, "we should have thought of that ourselves. His willingness or otherwise will clear up at least some of the problems. I'll be your assistant, Dr. Allen, if you need one."

"Sleeve up, Devlin," said Allen.

The man struggled to regain his calm. "As a matter of fact, I have already had an inoculation, and as you know, double doses are almost never recommended, and so far as I know have not been tested with this—"

"Come now, Devlin," said Allen soothingly, waving the needle with a reassuring glance. "Twice harmless is still harmless, but there is an urgent need for the demonstration. Get ready, please."

Devlin started from his chair and rushed to the door, heaving it open. At the open door stood the two impassive figures of Reid and Macfarlane.

Raeburn welcomed them heartily. "Ah, come in, friends. You may be able to give us a little assistance. We are about to give this gentleman a small inoculation, and he seems unduly nervous."

They entered, Macfarlane saying, "Well, now, there should be nothing there to worry anybody, especially anybody with a good conscience. What might be the best way now, sir, to go about the wee operation?"

Dr. Allen took it up. "He should be sitting in that chair and not moving much."

Reid said, "Weel, that should be richt easy." The two smooth performers acted, and in a moment Devlin was pinned on the chair, with Reid gripping his shoulders from the back, and the other standing by.

"Excellent!" Dr. Allen approached. "Sleeve up," he said again.

"No, damn you! No!" Devlin struggled until Macfarlane rested a finger hard at the corner of the jaw. Reid addressed Dr. Allan. "What's tha aboot the sleeve, sir?"

"He should have his sleeve up well beyond the elbow."

"That should be nae bother at a', sir," Reid said. Macfarlane already had a knife out, gleaming sharp and well used. With a grip on the left wrist, he stretched the arm out and cut away the cloth of the jacket sleeve and the shirt from just below the shoulder, tossing the cylinder of material into the wastepaper basket. "Would that be the way you wanted it, sir?" he enquired.

Allen nodded. "That's not the way we generally do it, but that will be quite satisfactory. Devlin, what is all this howling for? Don't we all know the serum is quite harmless, and of course the needle is sterile—it says so on the package."

"Oh, Christ, no!" he was beseeching. There was no chance of his struggling out of the grip of the two gillies, but his whole body was heaving and arching, and the voice cracked as he yelled in terror.

Allen was at his bedside best. "There now, man, it will be all over in a minute. I promise you won't feel a thing." He moistened a swab tenderly and rubbed it on the spot to await the needle. As he approached the skin, the man crumpled.

"Oh, Jesus Christ, don't do it! It would kill me. I'll tell you everything. Put that thing down, for God's sake." He was now sobbing and broken.

Raeburn said, "That sounds cooperative. When you say everything, I hope you mean everything. Dr. Allen, I think if you don't mind you should stand by with the needle, in case our friend is not as talkative as we would like."

"Happy to oblige."

"I suggest this is the drill, then. I shall take notes as we go along, and we shall also record the statements." He set up the tape machine. "Right, everybody? Then we'll start. I shall ask the questions, and of course the doctors can come in at any time, especially on the technicalities. Devlin, you're on. To begin with, tell us exactly who you are."

The story that came from Devlin was one of horror. At times he broke off to try to compose himself, but all the time Allen, hovering with the needle, stirred him into articulation again, and the narrative would resume. Devlin groaned to a halt at last.

Raeburn gathered up his pages and looked them over briefly. "Before we start," he said, "we could do with some silence from our storyteller. Not that I think he has sounded much beyond the room."

Reid casually wiped a wide strip of sticking plaster across the man's mouth, cutting his output to a mumble. Macfarlane had in the meantime dropped the limp arm and, walking to the window, rapped casually upon the glass. "Double glazing," he announced. "Clever idea."

"Right then?" said Raeburn. "Here is how it goes," and he started to read.

"His name is William Chalmers, born and brought up in Edinburgh. While still at school he was several times in trouble with the police, mainly on petty things like shoplifting and one serious assault. However, he had a good enough school record to gain entry to the medical school of the University of Edinburgh, where he studied, not too conscientiously, for four years. He was doing hospital work as part of his senior studies when he was detected in a series of thefts of drugs that he was selling to pushers outside, and for this he had a jail sentence. Fired from the university, he appears to have taken to a life of crime, picking up a few more prison sentences, for blackmail, fraudulent practices, and so forth.

"At some time recently he made contact with the late Lord Melfort. He claims to have operated for Melfort in a number of transactions, most of them more than dubious and some doubtless illegal. I think we can assume his story in this chapter is mainly true, for there is no doubt Melfort needed front men who would cover for him.

"Not long ago Melfort took him into his confidence in a matter I happen to know something about. He came here and told me that, working for a foreign power, he had been commissioned to put into their hands a very bright youngster called Michael Mackay. This lad is a genius in the field of electronics, and the foreign state wants him to man a long-distance spacecraft for as long as forty years or more.

"That has not happened yet, and the boy can probably be reckoned safe since he is leaving this term to attend a research institute in the United States. However, no doubt Melfort would have kept on trying if he had lived. He had built up great expectations on the Mackay project, and in a fit of madness he decided to bring the whole plot down with him, involving as many people as he could.

"This is where Devlin comes in. The scheme was entirely Melfort's, he tells us. The serum has nothing to do with hay fever and is very far from harmless. It is a preparation containing the AIDS virus, and if it had been administered to every pupil, it would have been a potential disaster beyond description."

Dr. Allen had long since laid the charged needle gently in the black case, closing the lid and clasping the locks.

Raeburn continued, "For all this, Devlin required an inside contact in the school itself. He tells us that the man is called Divito, who was recruited at the beginning of the term as a kitchen assistant. I doubt my cook-chef Ridley made many enquiries as to bona fides. Devlin tells us that Divito has some Red Brigade connection. We'd better assume that to be true. It was he who reported that the way might be clear for the administration of the inoculations, since Dr. Whitfield had gone away early for his holiday. Sheets of notepaper for the bogus health department letter were supplied by someone also working for Melfort, but again not traceable to the deceased. Quite a network, had the late lamented."

Raeburn looked up from the papers and turned to the trussed man, whose wrists were by this time tied neatly together behind his back. "Anything more, Devlin-Chalmers?"

The man mumbled from his throat, nodding his head violently. Reid tore the gag from him, and the voice immediately started its shaking pleas. "Oh, for Jesus' sake, don't kill me. I could go away. Disappear . . ." Reid clapped the gag back on.

"The next stage, then," Raeburn said, "is to decide what to do with this fellow. It seems to me to be a police job from now on."

"We can't avoid that."

"Not at this stage." The two doctors were in agreement.

Reid cleared his throat. "You'll maybe no' have remembered, sir, but the deputy chief constable is my cousin. The Duke himself has found that useful more than once, I can tell you."

Raeburn acknowledged him and said, "Fine, then. I think the drill is that Reid drives him to police headquarters and turns him in. They can come out and take statements from us here. I don't think any of the rest of us should leave the school premises. They'll no doubt get a statement also from this fellow—eh, Devlin?" There was a nod and a groan. "He can give as full a version as he likes. So far as we are concerned, all we know is that he turned up here with the inoculation scheme, we became suspicious, and after a little persuasion he confessed all. It's an offence to masquerade as a qualified doctor, quite apart from the murderous intention. He's no doubt wanted elsewhere on other matters. One way or the other, he can look forward to quite a stretch inside."

"He'll be safe for life from any retribution from his fellow thugs," Allen remarked. "By the way, what about the stuff?"

"Yes," Whitfield said, "it's highly dangerous. We'll hand it over carefully to headquarters. The police surgeon will know how to dispose of it."

Raeburn thought. "We're forgetting one thing," he said. "We'd better get onto this Divito right away."

"If you please, sir, I'll go down to the kitchen and bring him up here. He'll maybe feel like talking—after . . ." Macfarlane had drifted to the door and was lifting a gun. Reid followed and lifted the other gun.

"Good idea," said Raeburn. "Yes, bring him here. No rough stuff unless he won't come."

"Oh, he'll come." And Macfarlane was already away.

They installed the limp figure of Devlin into the passenger seat of the estate wagon which Reid had brought. He ripped the gag off his captive's mouth, saying, "If there's a cheep oot o' ye, laddie, ye'll mak the rest o' the journey senseless." He leaned out of the window to say affably. "It'll be oors before they get here from headquarters. That will gie Macfarlane time to set up some fishing for the doctor gentlemen. They'll be wanting a wee bit recreation efter a' that. There's some bonny fish movin' in the Ninian pool." He slipped the car into gear and moved off down the drive.

The others went back into the room, Raeburn saying, "I know what we could all do with after that. . . ."

The first shot exploded at that moment; the second, louder and harsher, a moment later.

The three, without a pause, were out of the house and running down the drive.

12

Just inside the headmaster's gate, Reid's wagon was slewed across the drive, as if there had been an attempt to evade some assault. Reid and Macfarlane, each with a ready rifle, were converging on the vehicle; Reid from the left, and Macfarlane from the right.

The house group rushed toward the two, and the pace was telling sorely upon the doctors, whose breathing had turned to wheezing. Mercifully, Reid called to them from sixty yards away, "Ye can tak your time, gentlemen. There's nae need to be hurrying, and running like that is nae the sort of thing for ye anyway. I wouldna' be surprised if ye did yersels an injury." He laughed encouragingly.

Macfarlane, with a voice that carried, had more information. "It's feenished anyway," he announced.

The doctors gasped to a halt, starting to walk with quaking knees. Raeburn loped on towards the wagon, on which the estate men were converging. "What the devil now!" he found himself saying.

"Ye may weel ask," Reid responded. The three waited until the others joined them. Then Raeburn said, "Tell us what you know. What happened? Who'll speak first?"

Macfarlane cleared his throat. "I would be thinking," he said ponderously, "it might be better if Reid started the tale. I'm kind of waiting to hear it myself. He was here first. I arrived a wee while later."

"But he was just in time a' the same," said Reid. "Anyway, there I was with the Devlin man aside me, and drivin' on towards the gate with no' a care in the world, when oot stepped a fellow from behind the left-hand gate pillar, a rifle in his hand and him wi' a bead on us. I swerved and at the same time tried to pick my gun up off the floor, but he shot straight and weel, getting Devlin through the middle o' the face. I haven't had more than a glance at him, but there's plenty o' mess where the bullet cam oot frae the back o' his heid. What was taking my attention at the time was that the fellow with the gun was now aiming at me too, but before I could raise my own gun there was another shot, and the man fell back amang the bushes. He'll nae get up by himsel', either."

Macfarlane put in, "Not likely. Through the heart, I would say, or as near as doesn't matter. We can check."

"Your story, though," said Raeburn.

"Oh aye, of course, sir. Well, as instructed, I went looking for this Divito. He wasn't in the kitchen nor in any of the stores, but a kitchen lass said she saw him leaving the premises only minutes before. He was carrying a gun and told her he was away to shoot rabbits; he seemed to be heading for the gate. I came down here at the trot, in time to give him what I would call the works, sir."

There was an interruption. A senior boy, followed by two or three others, was running towards the scene. He slowed when he saw Raeburn, and called, "We heard shots, sir. Is everything all right?"

Raeburn answered, "No problem here, Tony. A wee shooting experiment, that's all. All over—but thanks for the reaction. You can go back now."

"Will do." The boy marshalled his followers and led them at the run towards the distant main building. Raeburn watched them, saying, "That's Calder, the school captain. A sensible lad . . . Now, where were we?"

Whitfield said, "I think we were about to find out something about the second victim."

They went towards the scene. The man had tumbled forward into the low bushes, and only his feet projected. Reid hauled him out by the ankles, and with his own foot turned him over on his back, as he might move a culled roe deer. The man looked at the sky through his half-shut eyes, already dimming.

"That is Divito all right," said Raeburn. "Does anyone else recognise him?"

"Aye, it's him," the estate men agreed, with Macfarlane adding, "We have been getting acquainted with the school staff in the last two or three days, according to instructions."

Reid was pushing about in the recesses of the wagon and emerged with two tarpaulins, which he spread upon the grass. He and Macfarlane made a long bundle of the dead man. They hauled out the disfigured Devlin. "You gentlemen will have seen plenty of this kind of thing," was an aside to the doctors, and soon the two rolls were stretched together in the back of the wagon.

"Back to the house, everybody," said Raeburn. "It looks like the time for plan mark two."

"If there is one," Allen mused.

Reid stayed for a moment to lock the vehicle. "There's aye something," he remarked, as he caught up with the group.

Raeburn installed them in the big chairs round the room where he met occasionally with his heads of departments. Dr. Allen had seized on the rocking chair at once.

Opening the drinks cupboard, Raeburn told them, "Not a word from anybody until we've had something we all need." There were no refusals. Soon they were needing replenishment. Hovering above Reid with the bottle, Raeburn said to him, "You? You're driving, remember."

Reid held the bottle top briefly down over his glass, which became half full. He said, "I'm a gamekeeper. I can tak a helly a lot o' this stuff," and put the dram away in a swig and a half.

"Well then"—Raeburn had settled himself—"we haven't a great deal of time, but we've got to get this right. For a start, it seems to me that there's no way we can cut the police out. They'd better be in on this."

"That's for sure," said Allen.

"I'm wondering," said Whitfield, "if we shouldn't give serious thought to the idea of sending everybody home a few days early. For safety. Close the school. As the resident doctor I could probably invent something to say about it."

Allen shook his head. "I'm against that. The local government people, the press, the adjacent busybodies, would all come snooping. Parents would be interviewed, there would be endless speculation. No—that wouldn't work. I agree with the headmaster: At all costs keep the school out of it. We should try on our own to get through the day or two that remain until the official end of term."

Whitfield, pondering, nodded at last. "I believe you may be right. None of the pupils seems to be in any danger, except one. What's the drill about Mackay, Barry?"

"I think the Americans will send some sort of official escort to collect him. They'll advise us. In the meantime he seems safe, as long as he sticks to his tower."

"Any other complications?"

"A minor one. The BBC is sending a unit to do a documentary about how we do the end-of-term thing. I've promised them a fairly free hand to roam about. The term's work is finished, and this unit will be a diversion for the pupils."

Allen was dubious. "I never trust these chaps. They get into everything, filming away and always wanting more takes."

"Well, we'll see. Now, how about the bodies?"

"God, yes—the bodies! Same as before?" asked Allen.

"Why not? It's even simpler this time. Reid here trundles them down to police headquarters. They can be stacked in the mortuary. He gives a full statement, and in due course we can expect the police to turn up for a statement from each of us. This time all we say is that we rumbled the fact that Devlin was bogus, and were on our way to turn him in when his ally shot him, presumably to make sure he didn't talk. Divito was in turn shot by one of us in self-defence. Will that do?"

Whitfield said, "There is always the chance, of course, that the police might find that both of them had a record. Certainly Devlin had. Perhaps even an international criminal record. That would save us a lot of trouble."

Raeburn added, "Even better—if there is anything worthwhile in the international scene, MI5 or whatever would clamp down on the whole affair." He turned to Reid. "Ready for the road, then?"

Reid got to his feet. "If I'm lucky, I'll be back in time to have a go at the Ninian pool."

Raeburn told him, "On your way out, call to see Mr. Ridley at the kichens. I have instructed him to gather up all Divito's belongings and pack them up. The police had better have them."

They gathered to hear Reid's report when he arrived back from his errand. "It a' went according tae plan, sir. The twa o' them are safely tucked awa' on a shelf apiece in the mortuary, and by the time I was leaving there were reports coming in aboot ither villainies. I gied my tale. The cousin himsel' will be coming for statements from the rest o' ye, but so far it looks like routine. Of course, they ken Macfarlane and me, and we have long since been licensed to cairry guns. Twa harmless well-kent country loons, ye micht say." He and his crony shared a laugh.

Macfarlane was on his feet. "There's time for some real fishing. Take your rods, gentlemen. With the wind in this airt there's like to be an evening rise on the pool. Away we go, then."

He led the two doctors over the rise from which the brae dropped to the river. Reid said, "Lucky them. Ma' turn next. I'll just bide aboot the grounds and say a wee welcome tae any strangers that need discouraging."

He ported his rifle and set out. A good citizen, thought Raeburn, watching him go.

He quickly got rid of the more urgent of his routine duties, then sent for Rankine, telling him in outline of the state of the school's embattled affairs. Rankine listened intently and then went through the more obvious of the questions: Shouldn't they close the school early? Wasn't it a matter for the police? Was there any guarantee that the danger was over? It was all very well to avoid publicity, but would the whole thing not come out inevitably now that it was in police hands?

Rankine was ingenious in envisioning new perils as well as stressing the obvious ones. The exercise gave Raeburn the opportunity to rehearse his own conclusions, already reached. He found that his decisions grew firmer as his explanations went on, and he was not likely to waver from them. So they talked until Rankine appeared satisfied.

"Well, Barry," he said, "don't doubt me. I'm with you a hundred percent. Any hint in public of the things that have happened here would bring us crashing down. You do admit, though, don't you, that it is a huge risk?"

"I do. A fearful risk. It hardly bears thinking about. I have posted to a safe address a sealed envelope containing the whole story and exonerating everyone else, yourself included. If we succeed, I'll recall the envelope and destroy it; if we fail, I'll hand it to the authorities. That's final."

For the first time Rankine showed resentment. "Barry, you have no right to make a moral pauper of me. I've said I was entirely with you, and that includes carrying my full share for anything that goes wrong."

It had been a long time since Barry Raeburn had looked like the captain of a side hell-bent on winning. He had that look now as he faced Rankine. "It's my show and my blame, all of it. Nobody else's. If it goes down, you and the others still have a future. I'll have none. But I tell you, it will be a long time before I am able to say how much I appreciate what you have said."

They were interrupted by a shout from the hall. It was the voice of Dr. Whitfield. "Barry! Barry!" he was strident, like a schoolboy. "Come and see this. A miracle!"

As they ran through, there was the strangely penetrating voice of Macfarlane, saying calmly, "Ach, well, it would be too much indeed to say it was a miracle. It's maybe more a matter of knowing the right thing to do."

Laid out on the marble slab that formed the top of the entrance hall table were two noble salmon, fresh and still and gleaming. Macfarlane was hoisting them singly for weighing on a pocket balance. "One each," he declared, and there was no concealing the small triumph in his own voice. "Dr. Allen's is sixteen pounds, and now, Dr. Whitfield's is fourteen and a half." He laid the beauties tenderly back on the slab. "Not too bad an evening's work."

Macfarlane had produced two of the long baskets woven with wide straws, slipping the fish in and making for the door. "You'll want to take these with you when you go, gentlemen. They'll be waiting for you in the chill."

They sat long after dinner, while the two heroes rehearsed their tale with diminishing modesty. Headlights approaching up the drive sent Raeburn out to the front door. It was a sizeable van, with an unlit blue lamp on the roof. Policemen in uniform stepped out and started to unload gear.

One of them, with medal ribbons, shoulder badges, and silver scrolls on his cap, came forward with a hand held out. "Mr. Raeburn?" he said.

"That's me. And you are—"

"Reid. Davie Reid, deputy chief constable. I would recognise you easily, although it's been quite a few years."

Raeburn said, "You are here to take our statements?"

"Aye, that's right. The chief thought I should come myself with the squad."

"Quite a lot of you."

"Two officers with tape recorders, another two to take shorthand notes. One with the typewriter. An inspector. And the driver. It shouldn't take long."

There was no mistaking that he was a kinsman of the estate Reid. Sprucer, and erect, and likely as hard a man, with strong

Buchan undertones to a voice that had striven for a time to make itself intelligible to the people of Galloway.

Raeburn said, "Tell me what you need. I think we are all here —the two doctors, Allen and Whitfield, Macfarlane, who shares estate duties with your cousin. His statement will probably refer to a kitchen maid, and we can produce her if needed. Also some boys who heard shots. There were no witnesses as such."

"That sounds right enough. Can you give us two rooms, and we'll see you separately? Yourself first, sir."

The gear was set up in Jo Anne's room and a bedroom. The police chief presided in one room and the inspector in the other. It was a more thorough session than Raeburn had anticipated, for after he had run through his account of the affair since the arrival of the fraudulent Devlin, there were many supplementary questions, some of them covering exactly the same ground, some probing into such matters as what had aroused suspicion. Nothing was touched on concerning events before that day. The taped material was handed over to the man with the typewriter. "You will shortly have a copy of your statement to sign," said the police chief.

It was a long and late affair, and there seemed to be no way in which it could be shortened. Raeburn sat in his office while the others came and went. Allen was already waiting there when Raeburn was finished. The doctor said quietly, "An ordinary probe. There was no harking back." To which Raeburn responded, "You don't know the half of it."

"Just as well," said Allen.

When Dr. Whitfield returned, the same conspiratorial exchange took place. Allen said, "I think we can safely leave Macfarlane to be discreet," and Raeburn said, "Not much doubt about that."

It was necessary to rouse the school captain and the kitchen maid and to hear their stories. Raeburn was allowed, in the presence of the police chief, to explain to both that there had been a double murder and that all possible information had to be gathered.

At last the papers had been signed and the equipment gathered up. Raeburn walked to the van with the chief, who was saying, "You have been very helpful, Mr. Raeburn. This is not the sort of thing you would want Markland School to be mixed up in."

"I must confess to you, Mr. Reid, it would do us a lot of harm if any of this came out. For myself, I don't see any connection. Devlin's letter of introduction was forgery, although I suppose you will be clearing that with the local health department. I'd be grateful if in turn you would keep them and anybody else out of our hair."

Deputy Reid nodded. "I know exactly what you mean, Mr. Raeburn, although I can't give you any guarantees. All the documentation goes to the procurator fiscal, and he decides if there will be charges."

"Who could be charged?" Raeburn asked. "And for what?"

"Indeed, I'm beat to know myself. I doubt you'll hear anything more. And I don't think I'm breaking any confidence if I tell you that the two deceased gentlemen had criminal records over a long period and were wanted in more than one country. I wouldn't be worrying if I were you."

They parted formally. The school captain and the kitchen maid were plied with a small forbidden supper, and escorted back to their quarters, still excited, but ready to sleep, and sworn to silence.

Raeburn and his guests sat up, sharing the events. He persuaded them to turn in at last, then started to write some notes for remarks he wanted to make at the morning assembly.

There was the faintest tap from the heavy brass door knocker on the oak front door.

In the hall he leaned towards the door. "Who is it?" he asked.

A small, quiet voice said, "It's Michael Mackay, sir. Can I come in?"

13

In a single move Raeburn switched on the porch light and swung the heavy door open. Mackay stood on the steps, wearing the look of courteous diffidence and confidence he would undoubtedly carry for a lifetime.

He said, "I wouldn't have disturbed you, sir, but I thought it was important."

"Inside!" Raeburn bustled him in with a hand on his shoulder, heaving the door shut. As they stood facing each other in the hallway, the boy was wearing a sudden puzzled expression.

"Don't worry," the headmaster said, "never wise to stand in a lit doorway. Rogues and vagabonds about, for all we know. Come in."

In the office Mackay said, "You sound as if you had suspicions, sir. You could be right. I brought you something." He held up a small tape machine. "There's a tape here with some recordings I made about half an hour ago. I've been playing about with trying to see what odd signals I can pick up, and this lot came in on a wave that has never carried anything before, I believe. It might mean that somebody has something to hide. It mentions us."

"Let's hear it."

"The sound quality is very poor. I've written down as much as I can make sense of, and it might be easier if I read this first."

Mackay produced a sheet of paper. "Two men talking—a question first, '. . . name of the place?' Answer, quite clearly, 'Markland.' First voice again: '. . . easy to find?' Answer also clear: 'No problem. Name on gate. Pick up the cars at the map reference and follow them.' Then there is a very confused bit, something about painting vans, and '—dry by tomorrow.' Then a quite clear phrase: 'No response from Divito.' I lost the voices after that. They probably stopped transmitting. Would you like to hear the tape now?"

"In a minute." Raeburn went into the kitchen and came back with a can of drink and a hunk of cake, setting them down before the boy. "Get into that while I listen."

Raeburn could get nothing more out of the tape. He listened several times and said eventually, "I give up. You've wrung every possible coherence out of it."

"I'm used to electronic sounds." Mackay spoke through a mouthful of cake. "Can you make any sense of what we've got? Who or what, for example, is Divito?"

It suited Raeburn to look baffled. He then turned on the headmaster tone. "By the way, Mike, what are you doing still around at this hour?"

"Yes—I was supposed to be packing up, but then I thought of having a last fling with astrophysics. I have an old book there by a man called Grant on physical astronomy. Fascinating, his views on stellar theory . . ."

The headmaster cut him off. "Quite. Now it's time you turned in. Thanks for the tape." Raeburn escorted the boy across the grounds and saw him safely into the tower.

Back at the office, he tried to surprise the tape into yielding up more of its secrets, and pounced several times on the section with Divito's name. But he could learn nothing more.

He came back from the early morning run the next day to take a call from Jo Anne.

"Hullo," he said. "Why so early?"

"Bad conscience. Making up for my lazy day yesterday. Call for you. Police."

"Mr. Raeburn?" It was the voice he had somehow expected. "It's Davie Reid here. There has been a development in the case."

"Complications?"

"Not quite. Rather the reverse. Simplifications—so far as you are concerned, Mr. Raeburn. Something has happened that I had thought was a possibility, but I did not think it appropriate to mention it to you last night. The case has been taken entirely out of our hands here. The security people—you know who I mean —have moved in. They tell us to keep clear and to leave the whole matter to them, unless we have fresh information, which seems unlikely. I think you can exclude the possibility that you will hear any more about the matter. I thought you would be relieved to know."

"I can't tell you how grateful I am for your consideration," Raeburn said. "It would appear then that there is no danger of the school becoming involved.

"You can probably forget that."

Raeburn was smiling when he joined Allen and Whitfield, who were already installed at the breakfast table.

"Have you won something?" Whitfield asked.

Raeburn's explanations were interrupted by the arrival of the breakfast party from the kitchens. The cook-chef had come himself. When the meal was ready, he dismissed his two helpers with a lifted finger and said, "You two—wait outside.

"A moment, sir, if you please," the cook-chef said then. "The plates are hot, so nothing'll spoil. I had a telephone call this morning—a person asking to speak to Divito. I had to break the news that he was dead, apparently under violent circumstances. I was in the middle of offering condolences on behalf of the school when the caller rang off. He did not indicate where he was, or I should have called back. I did mention, however, that the matter was in the hands of the police."

Raeburn's eyes burned with disapproval. He stared at the man, his knuckles white, and his lips a thin line.

"Ridley," he ground out, "you had no right to take this on yourself. Who gave you authority to speak for the school? This matter has been withdrawn from our jurisdiction by the police and other authorities. It has complications that are beyond your comprehension. For all we know, this could put the reputation of the school at risk. Do you understand? Listen: Here is an order. You will not at any time, now or in the future, take it upon yourself to mention to anyone—anyone!—the death of Divito or any matter concerning it."

Ridley was stammering and staring. His self-assurance was gone, and it was some time before he could speak. "I . . . I . . . I . . . Understood, sir. I . . . Of course, the school, sir. Should have thought. Not a word—I'll remember. . . ."

"Take my advice and don't remember. Your job is to forget. Understood?"

"Of course, sir."

"That's all. You have work to do."

As soon as he had gone, Dr. Allen burst out, "Who the devil is that blundering blabbermouth?"

Raeburn groaned. "It's my fault. I should have remembered to turn off that faucet. He is Ridley, my cook-chef—good at his job, but dim, and the silliest gossip in the school."

He looked from one to the other, knowing that the three of them were already forming theories about fresh dangers. So there was silence until he said, "The trouble—the trouble is that if the call came from a relative or friend, the person would have at once panicked and been in touch with the police."

"Which he did not," said Dr. Allen crisply. "So that the call might not be described as an innocent enquiry."

"In sorting out the goodies and baddies," Whitfield put in, "it's clear that this Divito was the inside man. So the gang will know that he was rumbled."

Raeburn said, "It might mean that they'll call off any planned activity. Or they might move faster than they intended." He produced the paper on which Mackay had written the messages. Neither doctor was able to add anything to the frail meaning of the words. They listened to the tape and extracted nothing more.

The rest of the breakfast time was hurried, with occasional bursts of discussion. Raeburn said at last to Allen, "Well, that's it. Business as usual, and I'll be thankful when it's this time tomorrow. Dr. Whitfield and I are due shortly at the morning assembly."

They walked across the grounds to the assembly hall, which buzzed with conversation that hardly quietened when Raeburn walked down to take his seat in the front. The organ was playing softly. When it stopped, the chaplain stood at the lectern, and the hall hushed.

There was a brief prayer, a psalm, and then a hymn. The school captain read a lesson from the Scriptures, and a small boy sang a soprano solo. The chaplain stood again and announced: "The headmaster."

Raeburn looked over the tide of faces, recognising the several who would be going at the end of one more term. He smiled and addressed them.

"School," he said, "this morning's assembly has been a rehearsal for tomorrow's. In twenty-four hours from now we will gather for the last time this term. You all know your own travelling arrangements. In many cases parents will be coming to take you home. There will be buses for others to get them to railway stations or airports. Pupils in doubt about any detail should speak to their teachers immediately after assembly.

"Now here is an extra announcement. Some special visitors will shortly be arriving. The BBC is sending a camera crew to make a film about our end-of-term planning. They will have a free hand to go anywhere in the grounds, into classrooms and recreation areas—in fact, to film everything we do. They will probably pick out individuals for brief interviews—don't worry if you are chosen. It isn't an examination—and if you don't know the answer to any question, just say so. Heads up and speak out —no muttering. When you leave assembly, go back to your dormitories and put on your school uniform—clean shirt and school tie, best blazer, no fancy kit. As you walk about the grounds, don't look at the cameras. And when someone is being inter-

viewed, keep away. I don't want to see a background of idiots
waving and grinning.

"One more thing. Since we all have to get ready for leaving
tomorrow, we'll stay close to home for the day. Anything outside the school grounds is strictly out of bounds. Understood? I
think that's all."

The chaplain gave them a brief benediction, and they started
to file out, chattering. Raeburn stayed to watch them go. Allen
joined him finally in the empty hall, saying, "I won't be worried
when it's this time tomorrow."

"Agreed. Don't let's dwell on it. Time may be on our side."

In the office they awaited the arrival of the film crew, who
came shortly before midday: first a string of cars, and then three
great vans, with a few cars bringing up the rear. Raeburn went
to the front door to receive them. From the first car there
stepped a man in a casual jacket and jeans, who came forward
with a hand out.

"Todd Milligan. Producer and director both." He laughed,
well pleased with himself. In the meantime the cars were emptying and the forecourt was filling up with men.

"You have quite a crew here," said Raeburn. "Is that usual?"

Milligan said, "In fact, it's quite a small crew for this kind of
job. Three cameras and personnel—still camera, clapper,
makeup, reflector chap, script, van drivers—that sort of thing.
Nineteen altogether, more or less."

Raeburn pondered. "I'd have thought the BBC would have
advised me of the numbers involved—and, in fact, the names."

Milligan laughed again. "Good old Beeb! Our desk chaps
aren't very good at the bumpf jobs. Don't worry."

"I'll try not to. You will have some identification?"

"Sure. Here's my card—and, for good measure—" He
showed a plastic-sealed card with his photograph. "I wear this
when we do a high-security job."

"What I'd like you to do before shooting starts is to make a list
of all your people and the job each does," Raeburn said.

"Oh, wait a minute! Have a heart! That'll take a hell of a long time. Time is money, my friend."

"So don't let's waste it, then. You can use my office."

"I have my own office in the van here." He was testy.

"Good. Give me a shout when you have finished. Then I'll get one or two of the senior boys to show you over the grounds and the main classrooms."

"In fact, I don't need that. I have a map."

Raeburn sounded casual. "A map? Where did you get that?"

Was there a hesitation now? Milligan said offhandedly, "Oh, somebody at headquarters had a brochure about the school."

He climbed, grumbling, into the van, and the headmaster went to his office. Dr. Whitfield had joined Allen. Raeburn told them of the men's arrival and about the map.

Allen said, "Doesn't sound very suspicious to me. School brochures generally have a plan of the layout."

"I don't think we have a brochure like that," said Whitfield. "But I wouldn't know for sure." He paused, then nodded in the direction of the secretary's office. "She would know."

"Of course." Raeburn lifted one of his phones. "Jo Anne, will you please come in for a moment?"

When she entered, he said to her, "Jo Anne, you've been here for a few years. Did we ever issue a school brochure showing the buildings and, say, maps of the school grounds?"

"Definitely not. Your predecessor had a firm opinion on that. He would never take a pupil whose people had not visited the school." The outside phone on his desk rang, and she lifted the receiver. She covered the mouthpiece briefly, saying to Raeburn, "BBC Glasgow for you."

He said, "Raeburn here."

"Good morning. This is William Hamilton, programme director of BBC, Glasgow. Mr. Raeburn, we owe you a profound apology. It seems that—" The voice cut off suddenly.

Raeburn hung up. "Cut off. They'll probably ring back. Too bad. I'd a few things I wanted to ask about."

He turned to the others. "You can make yourselves at home here or in the house, whichever you prefer. I'll stay here. This is my headquarters anyway, and I don't want to be away while the film mob is around."

Allen said, "I think we want to sweat it out with you. Eh, Whitfield? The three of us had better be together if any balloon goes up."

"I'd feel happier that way," Raeburn said.

Jo Anne came in again. "Headmaster, I've got Michael Mackay waiting to see you. Is it all right?"

"Absolutely. Send him in."

The boy came into the office and at once looked hesitantly at the two others there. "I'm sorry, sir. I came to ask—but—"

"Sit down, Mike. You know Dr. Whitfield, of course, and this is Dr. Allen, another friend. They know all about you, and you and I have no secrets from them. What did you come to ask?"

"I hope it doesn't sound silly. I came to ask if I might borrow a large white sheet from the school laundry."

"Heavens, what for?"

"You'll probably think this is the silly bit. It's easy to explain if you will listen to another tape I have just made. Can I borrow the tape recorder I left here?"

The boy loaded the tape, and they bent to listen. "I should tell you first that I took this from a secret code channel used by the American forces.

"The voice belongs to a captain of the U. S. Marines, who is with a crew patrolling in an aircraft at a great height above us. He was on the air, operating through one of their satellites. The captain seems a cheerful gentleman, and he seems to be talking to his second in command. Listen now."

"—that big house down there—sharpen it up on the screen— is that Markland School where our whiz kid is? We'll pick him up tomorrow. . . . I wonder if he's bright enough to break the code. If so, he can hear me now. Why don't we see? Okay, then, here goes. Message starts. Hi, there, young Mackay. If you're as good as they say you are, you're hearing me now. To prove it, fly a white flag from the pole on that tower. We'll be dropping in tomorrow to fly you back. It's all cleared with your dad, and there will be an official message for your headmaster. We know all about the Dalshay mob, and I promise you they won't get you. Be seeing you, son. Message ends."

Mackay switched off the tape, saying, "If you don't mind, sir, may I have a white sheet?"

"Boy," Allen burst out, "you can have a medal." To Raeburn, he said, "A sheet, quick!" Raeburn was already hustling Jo Anne on the run to the laundry, with Mackay after her.

"That could be a real stroke of luck," said Raeburn. "With these marines watching over us, I don't see any other lot getting under their guard."

The three of them relaxed with relief, until Raeburn said, "I'll go down and see if Milligan has finished his homework."

The producer met him at the entrance and handed over a list. "Now," he grumbled, "are we to be allowed to get on with the job?"

"Certainly. Don't let me keep you."

"For a start, when do we get a shot at this boy genius you have? He went running past a minute ago, with a woman in a hurry. I have to tell you that we are in a hurry too." As they talked, a still-cameramen was pushing his instrument close to the headmaster's face and clicking.

"I'll take you to his workshop," Raeburn said. "Quite spectacular. You'll get good pictures."

Milligan waved to some of his crew, and three of them followed him as they walked. Milligan explained, "We need lighting, still camera, film crew, clapper—that's all—and me. You might tell me, by the way, who are those two tough country gents in tweeds who hover about. They've got guns."

"Don't worry about them," Raeburn assured him. "They are estate men. Always around. You could call them our security." He could see the white sheet already streaming from the tower flagpole. He opened the gate to the stairs and shouted up, "Mike —visitors for you." They heaved their gear up the stone steps.

He stopped here and there on the way back to talk to the groups of two or three or more who were strolling along the paths, striving to be calm and hoping to be selected. The remaining two cameramen seemed to be busy, shouldering their cameras and panning and crouching. One of them took a long shot of Raeburn approaching and entering the door of the main building. He did not have to pretend to adopt a purposeful pose. He had a purpose.

In his office he said, "All seems to be going smoothly. So far so good." In the meantime he had taken from a cupboard his powerful binoculars and was training them through the window at an object he had seen on his walk back from the tower. He focussed and brought the subject near and sharp.

It was an elegant female figure, sitting modishly on a bench in a bower of trees where rising ground led a path to the assembly hall. She wore a daring suit in purple, with the skirt an inch or two shorter than even the current fashion. Silvery stockings sheathed the long crossed legs, which ended in black high-heeled shoes. On the head was a beret, in white; and draped around her neck was a scarf in green silk. Huge earrings swung from her ears, and the hands, lying along the back of the bench, were crusted with rings.

The two doctors had by this time joined him at the window. Dr. Allen said, "Who is she? Is she in the script?"

Raeburn said, almost to himself, "I thought so." He handed the glasses to Whitfield, saying, "Do you see what I see?" He walked across the room and opened his secretary's door. "Jo Anne, please ask Miss Wilson to come and see me."

Dr. Whitfield had turned away from the window to say, "My God—it's unbelievable."

"Nothing," said Raeburn, "is unbelievable these days."

Allen had become left out of it, but he chimed in with, "What now? Mair ghaisties and lang-leggit beasties?" They did not respond until Pamela Wilson arrived.

She took the binoculars from Raeburn, who gestured towards the figure on the bench. When she turned back, her nose was pinched with anger. She said harshly, "Elaine Grandison! Barry, I'm angry now! I'll deal with this. Sitting there dressed like a tart!" She made for the door.

"A minute." Raeburn was following her. "I'd better be with you for the confrontation. After that it's all yours." He pulled the door after them and said to Whitfield as he pointed to Allen, "Tell him."

They walked fast and silently to the bench. There were no other pupils about, and a distant cameraman slipped away through the bushes. Raeburn left the talking to the games mistress, who said, "Home, young lady! You'll come with me, and I shall see you changed and scrubbed. On your way."

Elaine turned to them a face suddenly startled and frightened. And defiant. Her face was plastered with badly applied makeup.

"No, I'm not coming! You've no right—this could be my great chance. They'll discover me. I could have a film career. Go away!"

She was looking round in a passion of rage and frustration, hoping perhaps for rescue.

Raeburn said quietly, "Elaine, you know the rules, and you heard the instructions this morning. No exceptions. Miss Wilson will look after you. I shall see you later."

She blazed at them, "Oh, I hate you! And I hate this rotten school! My father will take me away from here."

"Probably. In the meantime, Miss Wilson, please get her out of here."

Pamela Wilson said to the girl, "Let's go. If you don't come, I shall lead you, and it will be painful." Elaine was sobbing now, the tears making sooty streaks in the thick makeup. But she went quietly at last. As they wound through the trees, he heard the games mistress say, "Anyway, Elaine, that makeup is a disaster, and I think you know it. You have a lot to learn."

Soon Miss Wilson came back to the office. She sat having tea, perfectly composed. "No," she said, "I'm not giving any detailed report. It's over. And there is a very smart schoolgirl, in a neat uniform, to be seen in the precincts." She took some bites of cake, and continued, "You know, headmaster, I think you might do worse, one of these days, than to think of getting someone to come in regularly to give the senior girls some tips on makeup and dress and hairdo's and whatnot. Just think it over. Don't ask me a lot of questions just now. I think you ought to know it can be hell to be sixteen and female."

The men nodded, but stayed silent until Raeburn felt bound to say, "Would it work, do you think?"

She responded with mild satirical emphasis. "Would it work!" Shortly afterwards she left them.

Dr. Allen said, "Amazing person. Sensible—and quite attractive. Are there many others like her in your profession?"

"We have some very good ones. All different. They rarely conform to pattern."

Jo Anne came in to report. "Headmaster—another snag. I tried to get back to the BBC, and there is no reply from the exchange. It seems that all the lines are out. The last time it happened it took nearly a day to get the connections going again."

"Jo Anne, find Reid and Macfarlane. They have walkie-talkies and will know how to get others. I used to have one myself. And see if you can find anybody in the technology department. Get them to rig up some small portable communication gadgets and bring them here."

"I really don't think," she said, "that you would have long to wait for a post office hookup."

"I'd prefer not to wait," he said. "Do you mind getting on with it?" She escaped.

One of the doctors was saying, "I suppose these BBC chaps could fix up something."

"I suppose they could," Raeburn said, "but somehow I don't think this is the time to ask them."

When a small tap sounded on the door, Raeburn was swift to open it. Michael Mackay stood at the entrance. He was breathless from running.

"I've got something to tell you, sir. First of all, Mr. Milligan didn't want me to leave the tower. I had to insist, saying I needed something from my locker in the dormitory."

"So what's been happening?"

"It all looks normal, sir. I have explained a lot of things and shown them experiments. They tape the sound and take still pictures."

"Well, that's all right, isn't it?"

"No, it isn't. These men are fakes. There are no tapes—films, you know—in their video cameras."

14

Ian Rankine was saying, "We have no alternative but to call in the police."

"No police." Dr. Allen was firm.

Michael Mackay had lost his deference. "Anyway," he said, "we have no way of getting in touch with them. The telephone lines seem to be cut. Sabotage. None of our walkie-talkie systems will carry even to the edge of the region."

"What I could do," said Rankine, "is get out my motorbike and rush out through the main gate. I could be at police headquarters in not much more than half an hour."

"No police—not yet," Raeburn said.

Reid had cleared his throat, and they listened. "You would have a gey poor chance o' gettin' tae your bike. I ken it's in the big garage, and they've a van parked in front o' the entrance, and a fellow posted—with a gun, like enough. Another at the main gate. We saw all this on the way up here. Anyway . . ." He looked at his companion, who took up the statement.

"Anyway," said Macfarlane, looking round, "we're better than policemen, us that are here. And maybe we could get the job done without shooting."

Rankine said, "I hope to God that's so!"

After the arrival of young Mackay, Barry Raeburn had gathered his allies cautiously at the headmaster's residence. It had taken some time to assemble them, but there they were, and so far there was no indication among Milligan and his gang that they had been detected. "Let's keep it that way as long as possible," he said.

"All right, then. What's first?" Raeburn was hustling them. "What's the order? We'd better get the priorities understood."

Michael Mackay was the first to speak. "Sir, I'd better get back to the tower. Otherwise they will be suspicious. I've been away a long time."

"You're right, Michael. If we can fend off suspicion for as long as . . ."

"God Almighty!" Rankine burst in. "You can't send him back there—"

Raeburn raised a hand to silence him, and looked round. "Any opinions?"

Macfarlane raised a hand. "It seems to me," he said, "that the boy here is safer than any o' the rest o' us. Is it not the case that they want him sound and alive?"

"That makes sense," Dr. Allen said. "He'll simply need to be innocent as long as possible."

"I'll try." Mackay was on his feet. "Could I have a screwdriver, sir?"

"A screwdriver? Why?"

Reid was at the door. "Tools in the kichen. I'll get one." He was back in a moment.

Raeburn insisted. "Why the screwdriver?"

Mackay said, "I said I was going out for something, so I need to have something to show. I'll let myself out. Thanks, sir." He was gone.

Reid pointed at Raeburn, with something like rebuke, and said, "When one like that asks for something, you get it. He knows what he wants. He'll go far." He turned away, abashed. "I'm sorry, Mr. Raeburn, sir."

A light tap sounded at the door. "I'll go," said Raeburn. Reid and Macfarlane followed him, their firearms coming automatically to their hands. The Duchess stood there.

"No, Barry, I'll not come in. No time to waste. I thought I should come for the girls. They'll be safe at Kintalla. The whole telephone system is down for two counties. What's the damage so far?"

"Nothing yet. We hope to keep it to the minimum. The BBC crew turned out to be phoney. They seem to be Melfort's mob after young Mackay. Not to worry. Full details later. I sent Pamela Wilson to collect the girls, meaning to take them in here. But of course Kintalla would be better." He peered into the deepening twilight. "I think I see them coming now. How did you get here, by the way? I think the mob has closed the main gate."

"There's an old disused gateway into the North Wood, over-grown and wired. I cut and bashed through it, got the car inside and out of sight, and walked down a trail to here. . . . Barry, can we get going? Tell the girls, will you?"

He herded them up the trail, saying, "No questions asked. It's a party. Follow the Duchess—and you too, Miss Wilson. Have fun!"

Over her shoulder the Duchess said, "I'll send you reinforce-ments. Take care, Barry."

From the anonymity of the little herd, one of the girls giggled, "Yes—take care, Barry."

Pamela Wilson's voice came fiercely. "Quiet there! No talk-ing." They quickly wended their way through the trees.

When Raeburn rejoined his team in the house, they were more animated, and Rankine greeted him with, "Barry, we've been thickening the plot."

"Please tell."

"Me first," said Whitfield. "As the school's doctor, I propose to take something on myself. We seemed to agree that the best circumstance for scuppering the kidnap plot during the night would be to have the school quiet, with all pupils sound asleep and unaware of any conflict or tensions. I suggest that I include in the supper porridge a mild soporific that will ensure a sound sleep for all concerned, and let the rest of us get on with the job."

Raeburn turned on him. "What?" he shouted. "Drug the lot of them? What's responsible about that?"

Dr. Allen said, "Calm down, headmaster. We are all with you. I agree with my colleague. If the children are in bed and sound asleep, they are out of harm's way. The drug is utterly harmless. A sensible idea. I hope you will agree."

Raeburn sat and looked round at the circle of nodding heads. He said at last, "Yes, I see the point. Sorry. Carry on. Do you want me to come and give Ridley the orders?"

"No, I should be able to do that myself," Whitfield said. "Doctor's orders. You'd better stay and hear what else has been cooking up."

Turning from the departing Whitfield, Raeburn said to the group, "What, then?"

Rankine said, "The bunker."

"The bunker?" Raeburn stared at him.

"Barry, you ought to know what it is. I've tried to show you over it, but you never seem to have time. Of course you have been tremendously busy . . ."

"Of course! The bunker—Scotland's last stand—"

"That's it. I don't think you have ever taken it seriously."

"Well, Ian, maybe now is the time. Don't be offended. To tell the truth, I thought I had my priorities right."

Dr. Allen said, "I like enigmas as well as anybody, but would somebody please tell the rest of us what's all this about the bunker?"

"Fair enough," Raeburn said, pointing to Rankine. "You tell."

"In fact," said Rankine, "some of us here know about this already. At the height of World War II, Britain was divided into defence zones that were to be self-contained in case of enemy landings and partial occupation. This part was selected as the focal point for operations if the country became divided because of invasion. A bombproof underground operations war room was established to house the command centre. Naturally, things are different now, but they keep the old one in good shape and more or less ready for anything. It's inspected three times a year. They were here a few weeks ago, and it has power and water."

Allen said, "Interesting. What's that got to do with our problem? Where is the bunker?"

"It's here," Rankine said. "The old mansion house, which is now the centre of the school buildings, was requisitioned during the war, and the bunker was built in the grounds. There is a large mound, covered with trees, which the old maps describe as the Giant's Grave—local belief being that there is an archaeological site of some significance. In fact, it is a glacial moraine—a huge heap of stones and rubble left behind as the ice melted. The bunker is dug into that."

Raeburn said, "That's the place for us. This house is too vulnerable if it comes to a showdown. How do we get into it?"

"I have a key," Rankine said.

"But all this is years ago." Allen was pressing the point. "The place must be crumbling and derelict—unhealthy. How do you come to have a key anyway?"

Rankine was reluctant to appear to be making claims of importance. "I'm a member of the local territorial force. They asked me to be a kind of contact man for the authorities."

Reid cleared his throat deferentially, saying, "We've a key and a'. At least his grace has one, and we ken where it is."

Barry Raeburn was on his feet. "Let's go," he said. They assembled in the small entrance hall as he turned out all the lights and opened the door. Standing on the step, with a hand outstretched to touch the door knocker, was Dr. Whitfield, with another figure dimly behind him. The two stepped in. Raeburn closed the door again and switched on the lights.

"What now?" he asked.

"I gave Ridley the order about the porridge, but he insisted on getting confirmation from yourself. Here he is. Speak up, Ridley."

The cook-chef said, "The porridge is cooking now, and will be served on time. But in view of the unusual nature . . ."

"You are right, Ridley. I confirm that an addition is wanted in the ingredients tonight. Quite harmless. Has it been done?"

"It has. I attended to the mixture myself, so I am the only one who knows. Unless my staff hear from me, the serving will go ahead as usual."

"Well done, Ridley. Come with us, then. Let's go."

They were clustered at the darkened entrance again when Raeburn suddenly spoke. "Quiet, everybody! Somebody coming."

Figures—three of them—were moving down the track where the Duchess had taken the schoolgirls. Reid and Macfarlane slid their rifles to the front. A sudden full beam from a torch held by Macfarlane splashed onto the face of the leading man.

"I know him!" shouted Raeburn.

"Ye may weel say that, Mr. Raeburn. I'm kent by maist o' the folk aboot here. But they'll no' be sae familiar wi' the big fellow I brang alang."

The torch beam had swung to the figure at his side; a man of great height, with shoulders twice as wide as the average. And he spoke up cheerfully. "Aye, Murdo, they dinna ken me, except maybe for Mr. Raeburn—but some o' them will likely hae seen me. They ca' me Hughie Beattie. I'm here daein' a wee job for Murdo Fletcher, an' it seems there's maybe a wee bit o' trouble where the likes o' me might be useful."

The big plumber stepped forward.

"You're wilcome, Hughie," Raeburn told him. "You won't get a cap for this—Markland isn't Murrayfield—but we might keep you busy. Who's the wee fellow at the back there?"

Murdo Fletcher said, smiling, "Speak up, lady, and identify yoursel' tae your freens."

Pamela Wilson stepped into the beam of light, with hands briefly upraised and shoulders shrugging. She said nothing.

"My God, Pamela! What are you doing here?"

She said, "The Duchess told me what was afoot, and I knew it was my kind of game. The girls are safely installed."

They crowded back into the hall, while Raeburn told the newcomers what might be happening. Aside, Dr. Allen took Pamela Wilson by the elbow, murmuring, "You shouldn't be here, you know. This will be dangerous."

"I hope so," she told him, detaching herself. "You don't know me."

"No," he agreed, "not yet."

"Time to go," Raeburn announced.

As they moved quietly to the door, Macfarlane was speaking into Raeburn's ear. "Reid and I were thinking it would be a good idea to put the film men's cars and vans out of commission. It's dark enough now. We'll do a double knock when we come back." The pair were instantly gone in the darkness.

Rankine led the way through the trees. At places, where the overhead canopy was thick, each held the jacket of the man in front. After about two hundred yards they were climbing the slope of the Giant's Grave.

He brought them to a massive steel door set into a side of the domed hill that had been cut away. They heard the key enter the lock and the oiled hinges give. A faint light came on. Rankine pulled some switches in the massive bulkhead wall. "Everybody inside," he said.

As the door closed, Rankine threw more switches, and the place was overwhelmed with light. A concrete ramp, ridged with footholds, ran in a curve down to a ground floor, where a great table sat ringed with chairs. Exits went off to other depths and tunnels, there was a gallery of stell round two thirds of the roof at the level of the entrance floor, manned with benches set opposite small sunken desks whose controls and scanning screens sat ready to come alive. The whole setting was poised to become a war room.

Rankine said as he went down the ramp, "Will this do, Barry?"

"I should say so. How about air conditioning? Although it seems fresh enough."

"I switched on the air conditioning as we came in, and it will stay on as long as we are here. But it comes on automatically every twenty-four hours even if there is nobody in residence. Water and drainage and electric power lines are deep underground. There are emergency fallbacks, but I don't think we'll need them."

"Okay then, everybody." Raeburn turned to his dazzled team. "Have a look round and see what you can find that might be useful. Meet in ten minutes."

Raeburn moved aside the large sheet protecting the table and took his place at the head, laying out the detailed maps he had brought of the Markland grounds. He had noted on them key points, measuring their distance in yards from the Giant's Grave. Murdo Fletcher soon tired of the exploration and took a seat with the fiddle he had brought, starting to tune up.

"Do ye mind?" he asked Raeburn. "I tak the fiddle wi' me everywhere I go—like a miner wi' his graith."

"Carry on. There's nothing like a tune. You must be thinking of an old-fashioned miner."

"I daur say. But there's naething auld-fashioned aboot a fiddler. We're aye bang up-to-date. How aboot a strathspey?" He snapped into one of the old dancing masterpieces.

Pamela Wilson emerged from somewhere, saying, "When does the assembly begin? Barry, I must tell you, I've just found the 'Ladies'.' Sumptuous! These wartime girls must have revelled. In fact, you might call it a boudoir. Rather better than anything we have at Markland."

"No envious remarks, if you please, Miss Wilson. You know —example to the young."

"I can see me strolling over here of an evening—"

She was interrupted by Ridley, who burst in, pink with excitement. He was wearing a tall chef's hat. "I say, headmaster, you've never seen anything like the kitchen. What equipment! And modern, too."

"Better than anything you have at Markland?"

"Eh, well, sir—I never was one to complain. . . ."

"Is there any food?"

"Food, sir! The kitchen is stuffed with it—full fridges and freezers—steaks, legs of lamb, chickens, pheasant, you name it. Dry goods, grain, flour, canned and preserved fruits, I could go on . . ."

"Well, don't. What about porridge?"

"Taken care of. A bag of lovely medium-cut Midlothian oatmeal, the best in the world."

"What about getting on with it, then?"

"First thing I did. It's cooking—ready in minutes."

By the time the team had assembled in the main hall, Ridley was elbowing his way through the door of his kitchen with a great tray on which sat the bowls of steaming oatmeal with cream. They sat to eat, or walked about, talking. There was the underlying elation and shiver of people knowing that some crisis was almost upon them and that there was no evading it. Raeburn said to Rankine, "I'm mostly worried now about young Mackay."

There came a double gonging tap at the steel door. "I'll go," said Rankine.

They heard his voice challenging quietly, and then the door swung open. Down the ramp came Reid and Macfarlane, with Michael Mackay between them. Reid had a plastic bundle in his hand, and Macfarlane was dragging the body of a man. He dumped the figure in a recess on the ramp, saying, "That'll be the first of them."

"Is he dead?" Raeburn asked.

"You might say he was in a deep sleep."

Reid pointed at Mackay. "We found this young fellow on the move aboot the grounds, looking for the lot o' ye."

"Better tell us all about it." Raeburn motioned them to seats at the table.

"It's a long story," said Mackay. "Do I smell porridge?"

They waited while the three ate, then Raeburn said, "Now. We're all agog. You first, Reid. What's in the bag?"

Reid tilted out some of the contents. "You could say they are trophies o' the chase. Distributors—one from each of the film crew's cars. They won't move an inch withoot these. As for the diesel vans—we took oot the batteries and hid them where they'll never find them. Ye might say that this gang is fair stranded. It was easy enough, for they mostly all seem to have gathered in the tower—except for this fellow here—" He thumbed towards the senseless man. "He was sleeping in the cabin of one of the vans. Likely enough he was on guard duty. There's a joke for ye! Anyway, he'll no' wake up for a while. We gied him a double roe-deer shot in the backside." He took a flat pistol from inside his jacket and laid it on the table. "This is a stun gun. We use it for putting the forest animals to sleep, so that they can have treatment. That was us feenished for the moment, except to pick up young Maister Mackay and bring him in."

"A good night's work—so far. Any questions?"

Allen said, "The stun gun is a good idea. It might be the way to deal with the rest of them."

"Might be—provided we can get near enough. They're probably armed. Michael, your turn."

"Sir, can I start by saying they are not armed. Well, not much. I'd like to tell it in the order it happened."

"Carry on."

"I left your house to go back to the tower, and when I got there Mr. Milligan was waiting for me, very angry. He shouted for a while—where the hell had I been? I wasn't to leave the tower again unless he came with me. Didn't I realise he was responsible for me? I told him I didn't, but he wasn't really listening. When we got to my operations room, I realised that they weren't even attempting to film anymore but were busy dismantling the apparatus. They were making a clumsy job of it, too, so I showed them the screwdriver I was supposed to have gone to collect, and I helped them to get the apparatus dismantled and pack it securely into boxes. I had really finished with that part of my experiments anyway. What they didn't know, of course, was that I had built into the sensitive parts of the signals receiver a self-destruct mechanism, so that whoever tried to put the thing together again would blow out the ion cells.

"Well, after that, he had a lot of questions to ask me. Most of them he didn't quite understand. I won't bore you with details, but it was clear he was informed that a certain powerful government was working on a project for a very long-term probe far into outer space. Something that would last for most of a human lifetime. It seemed that I was to be part of this. I didn't much like the idea. Anyway, I gave him some of the answers he seemed to be expecting, but I'm pretty sure he wasn't making much sense of them. About how a long-distance probe of that sort would use systems to bombard remote star and planet surfaces with laser and other beams to analyse soil composition, scan surfaces, measure rock composition with spectographs, probe the interior with radar—all that sort of stuff—by which time, of course, the technology would be moving on fast and would be being relayed to the probe. So that all the time they would be able to go farther and longer. . . . Sir, I've simplified it as much as I can. That's only the gist of it."

"Go on, Mike. It's the gist we're interested in. What happened next?"

"After that it was pretty ordinary. You may have noticed that there is a trapdoor in my operations room, which leads up to a small attic room. They shoved me up there, with Mr. Milligan saying something like, 'You'll bloody well stay there until we are ready to get going.' They shot bolts from the underside. I could hear them gathering in the room below. You can hear them too, sir; I was recording them through cracks near the trapdoor."

Mackay brought out from an inner pocket a slim tape. "I haven't heard this myself. Do you mind?"

He helped himself to one of the recording instruments with which the chamber was lined, clipped in, and waved them to silence. A voice came from the speaker. "That's Milligan," said Michael Mackay.

The voice was saying, ". . . got the Dalshay kid safe here. . . . wait until first light. . . . Got to find the headmaster's mob, they're not in the house. . . . Have to put them out of action. The pickup is south of Newcastle, so we need a good start. . . . men on the main dormitory doors—nothing moving there . . . bring everybody in here for instructions. Scout about for any place they might be holed up. There's nothing like that on Divito's map. . . ." The recording merged into a jumble of sound as men moved and jostled.

Raeburn said to Mackay, "But you haven't told us how you got out."

"Easy. A long time ago, when I first got the use of the tower, I hid a rope behind the panelling. I'm afraid I used it to make an occasional exit, sir. There is a sixty-foot drop to the flat roof of the first floor, but I got good at getting down and up again. This time I got down—I suppose for the last time. Once on the ground, I went back to the front door, hoping I could lock them all in. But they had taken out the key. Just inside the entrance there was a large box, full of automatic pistols. I carried it away. It was heavy. When I got to the old well in the front courtyard, I tipped the whole lot in, box and all. There was a nice spludge as the things hit the mud. Coming away from there, I met Mr. Reid and Mr. Macfarlane. That's nearly all, sir, for now."

"Any questions?" Raeburn said to the gathering. They laughed, some with relief.

Mackay spoke again. "I should have said I left a transmitter near the cracks in the trapdoor. The signals may be obtainable here."

"That's useful, Michael. We'll be able to tell when they start to move out of the tower." Raeburn said.

Mackay was already in the top gallery, fingering the apparatus, donning headphones, hooking up and tuning. They left him to it when Ridley came bustling through the door, saying importantly, "Dinner shortly. Smoked salmon for starters, followed by steaks. Anybody present object to steaks?" He backed out again, not waiting for an answer.

By the time they had drawn their chairs in to the table Ridley was already serving the first course. Murdo Fletcher took his fiddle and marched twice round the table, playing "Blue Bonnets over the Border." Michael Mackay set up on the table a receiver with two separate loudspeakers. Bottles of wine appeared. They all drank to Ridley's health and started in.

"I must say, Mr. Raeburn," said Macfarlane during a pause, "this is the kind of war that I like."

Afterwards Raeburn spread on the table the maps of the Markland grounds based on the six-inch-to-the-mile ordnance survey. "You'd better all gather round and study this," he told them. "Once we go out to catch up with our visitors, you'll have to be familiar with the terrain. Every clump of bushes is marked, nearly every sizeable rock, and of course all the buildings and the old ruins."

Reid said, "In a wee while it will be fair good moonlight."

"That will help."

Occasional fragments of speech came from the tower, where Milligan and his people were still dismantling. "That's the main screw. Try it." And "No—it's this one." They fumbled on for an hour.

Finally Milligan was saying, "That's it. Get everybody up here." Footsteps were heard, and there was a growing swell of voices. The hubbub hushed as Milligan started to speak. In the war room they poised to hear, hardly breathing.

"Gather round, then, fellows. We're ready to take off. Everybody knows what he has to do. This gear goes into my car, and

Manson will follow me in his in case of a breakdown. You know where the rendezvous point is. We must be airborne at latest fifteen minutes after I arrive. The others will scatter as agreed. Your money will follow by ordinary post. There must be no attempt to communicate with each other or me at any time. Anyone who talks now or later will get the chop. You'll not hear anything until the Dalshay mission gets going. I don't expect many of you here will still be alive when it finishes.

"The kid goes in my car. Get him down, Manson. We'll have to tie him up and gag him."

There was a near explosive knocking at the trapdoor, and a voice shouting, "Right! Time to go."

Michael Mackay smiled to the ensuing silence. The voice of Manson shouted again. He seemed to pull a table below the trapdoor, and they heard the bolt being sprung. The man's head was close to the transmitter as he shouted, "He's not here!"

"What the hell do you mean—not here!"

The scrambling noise was Milligan pushing up into the attic. "Christ, you're right. He's gone! He had a rope, the little bastard!"

The listeners heard them drop to the floor below, and Milligan was tense as he tried to overcome his rage.

"After him! Get him! Anyway, anyhow. Bound to be on the grounds somewhere—he can't get into the dormitories. Keep contact with your walkie-talkies. When he is bagged, assemble at my car. Your guns are at the tower entrance. Pick them up as you go."

There was the sound of the footsteps on the stair, and soon remote shouts of "Guns—where? Who moved . . . supposed to be watching—"

They were all swarming into the tower now. The panic grew until Milligan called them together again, this time at the entrance. The voice was too distant to register.

"We'll give them time to get scattered," said Raeburn. "It would be sensible for them to form a line and sweep the place, but I doubt they are cool enough to think of that just now. Can you find any of the walkie-talkie signals, Michael?"

"I'll try," he said. For some minutes he switched among the dials, saying, "It shouldn't be too difficult. They're certainly using some special wavelength. Hold on—this might be . . ."

Milligan was saying, "—too many people talking. Keep speech down to a minimum. Essential signals only. Get going."

Raeburn said, "Keep that, Michael—you are the signals department. Stay with it. The rest of us had better get out there and start the counterattack. Ready all?"

"Before you go, sir—will you give me just a moment to try something?"

15

Mackay did not wait for permission. He bounded up the ramp, rummaged among the gadgets, and was back at his place at the table holding another instrument. Headphones on, he barked, "Silence, everybody, please! Just a minute for this."

They stood like waxworks, even their breathing quiet. He had switched off the speakers, but an uplifted finger showed that he was receiving Milligan's signals in the headphones.

At last he said, "I think that's it. Sorry for the holdup." He turned to Murdo Fletcher. "Mr. Fletcher, would you mind playing the note of B flat and holding it?"

"Nae problem," said Fletcher. "Holding it for how long?" The bow bounced on the string, and the note came, steady and clear.

"Difficult to say. Twenty minutes at least. Quiet now, please."

"Good God!" Fletcher grimaced, holding the note. They all watched, still silent. Mackay was busy at the controls, intent. He spoke again to Fletcher. "Can you put it up a quarter tone?"

The man grumbled this time. "Who the hell dae ye think I am? Yehudi bloody Menuhin?"

"Quiet again, please." The boy listened and adjusted busily and said, "That's it! Perfect! Keep going."

Fletcher said, "If only I kent what's going on."

Michael Mackay removed the headphones and said, "It's a matter of simple mathematics. Most people know that radio signals, as well as musical notes, are a matter of how many vibrations per second. This sound"—he gestured towards the fiddler —"is exactly on the wavelength of Mr. Milligan's walkie-talkies, so that it will be able to render their radio speech impossible. The note will cancel out their communications totally. We have a transmitter somewhere in an adjacent tree. I shall put this microphone beside the violin, and Mr. Fletcher is broadcasting and, incidentally, sabotaging the signals. Keep it going, please, Mr. Fletcher."

"Ye mean I am on the air?"

"You are indeed, sir. Loud and clear."

Raeburn said, "Fascinating. Can we go now, Michael?"

The boy nodded and grinned. As they set off up the ramp, it was Ridley, emerging from the kitchen, who scrambled after them. He was carrying a basin full of kitchen implements. "Gentlemen," he puffed in pursuit. "You must not go unarmed into the conflict. I brought you a selection of items from my store—rolling pins, potato mashers, steel ladles, carving knives, choppers—that sort of stuff."

Some of them raked self-consciously among the selection and chose the thing they best fancied as a weapon. Dr. Allen flourished a wooden implement shaped like a mason's mell.

"See this?" he said. "It's for mashing potatoes. My granny had one. She called it her tattie beetle. I used to play with it, pretending I was attacking the giants. Now's the time!"

Others also claimed that their granny had a tattie beetle. One said to Ridley, "Is that the only one you have?"

They were ready to go. Raeburn said to Pamela Wilson, "Of course, you are not coming, Pamela. You are in charge of headquarters here. Let us in at a double knock, and somehow make sure it's one of us. Ready?"

Dr. Allen said to the woman, "Miss Wilson, do take care. No need for you to go outside."

She slid the door open and shut it firmly behind them, saying only, "Good hunting!" She went down to the floor level where Mackay and Fletcher were busy. The fiddler was sawing away on a sound that appeared to be losing its musical appeal, and the boy was still busy among his gadgets.

"What are you doing now, Michael?"

"Easy, Miss Wilson. I'm going to let Mr. Fletcher off the hook. He's been holding that note for ten minutes, and I think that is about plenty. I have been recording him on a tape loop, and I think it's enough to broadcast continuously. He can stop . . . just five seconds more . . . give me time to get the tape on to the transmission. There, that should be it. You can stop now, sir. It was a fine, steady performance."

"No' a great variety program." Fletcher dropped his bow arm gratefully and briefly sucked his strings finger. "Am I off the air?"

"Until further notice. Thank you very much."

Miss Wilson said, "What do we do now, then?"

Mackay was writing in what looked like a logbook. "Must keep the timings in proper order. There!" He finished. "I must have the door opened, to make sure the tape is sounding all over the grounds. Do you mind, Miss Wilson?"

"If you think it's necessary. I'll come with you; you must not go outside alone."

At the top of the ramp she first opened the door a crack and then more fully. They listened. From the unseen speaker the tone of Fletcher's fiddle was moaning through the air.

"Good—that's fine," said Mackay.

"Quiet!" she said. "Somebody's coming."

A figure, ill-lit by the late-rising moon, was heaving up the slope. As it neared, it seemed to be an enormous man heaving along two sacks of garbage, one in each hand. Pamela Wilson was swinging the door shut when the boy said, "Wait a minute— it's Mr. Beattie."

Hugh Beattie leaned into the open door. "Aye, it's me," he said. "Ye can shut the door now."

He was dragging the unconscious bodies of two men, whom he stacked tidily at the inner wall of the ramp, alongside the man who was already there. They were recognisable as members of the bogus film crew. Beattie flailed his arms to make them flexible again and drew some deep breaths by way of recovery.

"It was easy," he said. "I just went straight to the door of the big dormitory and found these two heroes who were supposed to be on guard. I heard them talking in a way that seemed tae indicate they had lost enthusiasm for the hale scheme. Anyway, they didnae hear me. I just grabbed the baith o' them by the collar and banged their heids together. Once was enough. I set aff for here, dragging them alang, and on the way yon two gamekeepers met me, and they gied them a stun gun shot in the backside. I didna ken when they'll waken up, but they'll have sair heids and sair bums."

"Something coming in," Mackay was saying from below. They joined him. He had set up the speakers again, and they heard the voice of Milligan.

"Manson! Manson!" he was saying. "Come in, Manson. Are you carrying your spare walkie-talkie? Come in."

"Manson here. Yes, I have it."

"Good. They are set on a different wavelength, and they can operate through this damned interfering noise. Meet me right away at the middle van. I have a gun for you. I had two spare ones under the dashboard of my car. Make it fast. Over and out."

"What now?" Pamela Wilson was truly worried. "Our men don't know that these two will be armed. There's no way we can let them know."

Mackay's hands were poised over his switches. "I can interrupt the violin note for a few seconds to send them a warning. Miss Wilson, can you think of how we should word it?"

"I'll announce it. Give me a moment." She took the microphone from the boy's hand and signalled him to switch off the sustained note. Immediately she spoke, fast and clear: "Attention, Markland men. Two of Milligan's men are armed—concealed guns. Be careful." She signalled again, and Mackay threw the switch over. Even in the depths of the bunker, their ears long attuned, they could hear faintly the dismal note of the tape as it began its endless coronach.

"Six and a half seconds," said Mackay crisply, putting aside a stopwatch. "Very good, Miss Wilson."

"If you say so." She was busy, tense, among the maps.

The two doctors, Allen and Whitfield, huddling in the lee of the roots of a fallen tree, nodded dimly at each other through the mirk. They had decided to hunt together. It was Allen who had claimed he could not run, and Whitfield had eagerly agreed.

"I must admit the gun has it over the tattie beetle any time," Allen said. "But it's time to confess I had a good rummage through the medical department in the bunker and was happy with what I took away. You were doing the same. What did you get?"

"You first."

"I'm old-fashioned. I took a few pads of cotton wool and some breakable phials of chloroform. Tighten the fist suddenly, hold the lot over the nose and mouth of the patient, and he's away."

"Good enough! Not quite so effective as my lot, though. I was a junior anaesthetist for two years in St. William's. I've a case here with needles of Grober's Chemo. One jag and they're bye-bye—for as long as necessary."

"Very efficient. Maybe it's time I was doing a wee sabbatical—to catch up."

Whitfield spoke reassuringly. "Allen, I don't know that you're missing all that much. What you *are* missing, however, at this moment, is the sight of the fellow creeping up on us from the top end of this fallen tree. He seems to know we're here."

"By God, yes!" Allen was peering. "I see him, and I see what looks like a gun in his hand."

They both watched the stalking figure edging his way down the tree trunk and pushing the branches noisily aside. The moonlight caught the shine of the weapon in his right hand. A wispy cloud, vanishing suddenly, gave a flash of brilliance to the scene.

"Time to try him out," said Allen. "Let's see if he can shoot."

Taking the tattie beetle, he put his cap upon its mell end and pushed the dummy beyond the fallen root.

The shot was quieter than they had expected, but Allen felt the thud as the bullet struck into the wooden head of the masher. He let the decoy bow helplessly towards the earth. As the gun-man bounded forward to claim his victim, Whitfield was there with a swinging foot that kicked the weapon out of the other's hand and swept it into the trees. He plunged a charged needle into the man, who was weakening already as they fell to the ground. Allen was on them at once, the sodden pad of cotton wool thrust into the man's face, and the two doctors held him as he went limp.

"Not too bad," judged Whitfield. "Out for some time, I'd say. Which one of us will do the surgery?" They laughed gently, still shaded by the upheaved root.

A human wraith became real beside them as Macfarlane rose from the far side of the tree. "Just me, gentlemen," he said softly. "You did well. I was coming to see if you needed help, but I might have saved myself the trouble." He turned the fallen man with his foot. "What have you done to put him so far away?"

"Medical stuff only," Dr. Allen explained.

"Oh, it's a great thing, medical knowledge. But I think I'll just give him a wee shot to make sure. That's what the others got— the double roe deer—and there is nothing like consistency." He turned the man backwards again with his foot, and the stun gun spat softly into his buttocks. "There, now—tidy and neat. Can you manage to take him to the bunker? I'd better be on my way. There will be other clients in the grounds."

They dragged the man up the soft slope and gave the knock at the steel door. Pamela Wilson opened it, and they heaved the man in.

Before they had finished with their story, the door boomed. This time it was Hugh Beattie back again, and without a word he stacked two more men onto the pile.

"It's almost too easy," he announced. "I got this pair at the door of the other dormitory, keeping watch the same as the others, and nae better. I wasnae sae successful this time with the heid banging, for one o' them lifted his heid at the wrong time and I doot he got his nose smashed. Weel, that was his bad luck. Had we no' better tie them up?"

Pamela said, "I've arranged that. Ridley, the chef, will do it. It's in his line."

At that moment Ridley came from his kitchen. He was carrying a frying pan containing rolls of heavy insulating tape, and as they watched him he strapped the hands of each man behind him. It was an expert job, for the chef in his time had trussed many a chicken and suckling pig. They left him to it, while they gathered again at the maps.

Ridley went on briskly attaching his bonds and came to the latest arrivals. He finished with the senseless man and did not notice the stirring of the other. The man with the ruined nose lifted his head, opened his eyes, and was reaching inside his jacket for a knife, which he then drew.

"Watch it, Mr. Ridley!" shouted Michael Mackay.

Ridley whirled with the reaction of a scared man and saw the danger. His practised hand closed on the handle of the frying pan, and he landed a blow on the man's head. The sound made a gong-like knell in the cavern of the bunker, and the man was again stretched out senseless.

Beattie, running up the ramp, had reached the scene, where Ridley was white and shaking.

"By God—ye did weel, cookie," Beattie told him. "Ye're a smart hand wi' the frying pan. I wouldnae wonder but you could make a living at it. Strap him up too."

Ridley had lifted the knife. "Do you think I could keep this?"

"I'm sure of it. He'll no' need it again, and it's nae use tae me, seeing knives arenae wanted on the football field—no' yet, anyway."

Ridley was pink with accomplishment as Beattie clapped him

heavily on the shoulder. Pamela Wilson interrupted them from the ground floor, calling, "Any sign of Mr. Raeburn out there?"

Beattie answered, "Sorry, I didnae see him. I was kind of busy masal'. I expect the gamekeepers are keeping an eye on him. If I come across him, I'll tell him ye were askin'. 'Bye-bye the noo," He let himself out, and the gate closed solidly behind him.

Barry Raeburn had business of his own. At that moment he was prowling the neighbourhood of the smaller dormitory, noticing that there were no guards on the door.

But he stiffened with apprehension to see a light glinting from within the building. It was moving and seemed to be making no attempt at concealment. He slipped to the door and opened it gently; he closed it behind him, standing still.

There was a discreet roar of water from the ablutions, and a figure stepped forth, making for the row of small cubicles that were the private studies of the senior male pupils.

"Stop there!" Raeburn commanded. "Not another step! Shine the torch on your face."

The beam moved upwards at once, and the face of Tony Calder, the school captain, was looking at him. The boy spoke coolly. "It's Calder, headmaster. I recognise your voice. Sorry to be a nuisance. Have I disturbed you?"

"We'll see. Light me to your study. I want to talk to you."

Inside the room, Raeburn checked the closed shutters, saying, "Switch on, Tony." The light in the small space dazzled them both for a moment. Raeburn took the only comfortable armchair, and Calder sat on the edge of the bed.

"Tell me—what are you doing up at this time of night?"

"Simple, sir—call of nature. Not unusual with me these days."

"I thought you would have been sleeping."

"I think I was only about half asleep—maybe thinking about end of term. I have a lot of duties to get through tomorrow—today, in fact. Then I thought I heard a kind of bang—like a shot. I lay in bed for a while but heard nothing more. Then I realised I had to get up."

"Tell me, did you have porridge last night?"

Calder was mildly uncomfortable. "As a matter of fact, I didn't, sir. I've been troubled recently with a touch of acne, and Dr. Whitfield suggested I might try dropping the porridge intake—heats the blood, or something."

"Okay—he could be right. No harm done. Listen, I have a job for you. First I have to tell you something you won't believe."

As Raeburn told it, the school captain's eyes widened in amazement. And when he heard at last, "That's it," Calder burst in with, "You mean here? You mean they're still here?"

"Here and now. I know only too well I'm responsible for you, but there is something I can't quite manage by myself. Will you come with me?"

The lad was on his feet at once. "I wouldn't want to miss this! Where to?"

"First of all, get your track suit on, and trainers. And do you happen by any chance to have an extra pair of shoelaces for me?"

"Of course. I noticed you have no laces. More than one pair?"

"Yes, bring them. I'll show you where mine went."

They left the dormitory silently, walking off gravel to reach a brake of low bushes. In a well-lit clearing what looked like a giant slug lay heaving and twisting. The two looked down at the man.

Calder said, "Is this the chap you knocked out? He's enormous. What did you do to him?"

"I gave him the chop behind the ear—twice. Maybe not enough. He's coming to."

"Another chop? Two more?"

"Not yet. We'll tie his hands and feet more securely. That's my handkerchief he's wearing as a gag."

Calder went to the job eagerly. He was in the mood where nothing would surprise him.

Not even the silent appearance of Reid, the gamekeeper, who came ghostlike through the bushes. "I saw ye dealing wi' this man and guessed ye werenae needing help. It was a tidy job. But he'll need a wee jag tae keep him quiet." He bent to the man's rear, the stun gun ready. It coughed once, and the figure heaved and made noises.

"It'll tak a while—just seconds—afore he settled doon quietly. A bit of a heave getting him tae the bunker. I doot I'll no' be able tae help. I might have a few customers needing me." He turned to go, then faced them again. "Oh, and something else, Mr. Raeburn. Mainly good news. Four of them have run for it. I saw them. They took a car from the staff car park and made aff like the hammers. They'll be easy picked up once we get on tae the police."

"Good! That's four less. You said mainly good news."

"I did. The wee drawback is that it was your car they took. I wadnae worry if I was ye. It'll be easy found. Like enough near a rail or a bus station." He slipped into the dusk, blithely.

Raeburn said to the school captain, "You take his legs, I'll take the shoulders. It will be a long peg to the bunker." They heaved the man up and started to move.

"I'm looking forward to seeing this bunker," said Calder. "Fancy it being there all the time."

"Save your breath. Keep going."

It was a struggle all the way. They had to put the burden down twice and then thrust on again. At the foot of the Giant's Grave mound, Macfarlane came from the trees, saying gently, "I thought it was yourself, Mr. Raeburn. I was watching you coming. Put him down. Who is he?"

"One of Milligan's lot. That's all we know. And a heavy one."

"I can see that." Macfarlane had out his stun gun. "Has he had the treatment?"

Raeburn told him about Reid's appearance and the double roe shot. Macfarlane said, "That's good. We don't like to be wasting ammunition. Give me a lift up with him—on my shoulders."

"But, man, look at the size of him. You'll never manage."

"Away with you! Lift!" They heaved the gross form onto him, and he hitched it into place. "He's not so heavy as a two hundred-and-twenty-pound stag, and he's even a wee bit tidier. Away we go." He took the slope almost at a run, the bent knees speaking of long hill travel.

Pamela Wilson opened the door for them, and Macfarlane dropped the weight on top of the heap already there. "There will be quite a cairn of them," he announced, "before the night is over." He had his gun out again. "Have they all had their sleeping draught?"

Ridley, presiding importantly over the fallen, singled out the unattended, and the gamekeeper did the work. The chef said to Raeburn, pointing to one recumbent skull, "That's mine." He held up the frying pan and told his tale.

Raeburn was warm. "Well done, chef! When this is over we'll get a suitable inscription engraved on the pan, and you can have it as a trophy. No explanations, though!"

Pamela, standing near, said to Raeburn, "We were worried about you. Have you seen anything of the good doctors? They came in with a prize and went off again. Hunting in pairs."

"Not a sign. Not to worry, though. They're a pretty adequate pair—professionals, you might say. Let me out, Pamela."

"Take care!" she said, and closed the door after him. And Macfarlane pushed past to reach his side, saying, "I'll better be on my way too. This is no time to be holding back."

At the foot of the slope, Macfarlane veered away from him with a word about finding Reid. Raeburn passed the front of the dormitories, ensuring that there were no lights on or any stirrings within. From there he zigzagged his way through the grounds, walking quietly and hearing no sounds.

Not until the bush clumps that marked the start of the low rise towards the assembly hall. Here the sound of struggling voices stopped him, and the sight of a writhing bundle of bodies. He peered closely, to guess which were his allies and which were his enemies. There seemed to be a central figure, still on its feet, and two clinging and heaving to bring him to the ground. Raeburn's eyes, now used to the half dark, saw that the upright man was Ian Rankine. Raeburn charged like a bull and brought the group down. He found himself choking the life out of the man who had been mounted on Rankine's shoulders and who now grappled vainly against the headmaster's hands. Rankine had turned to fight the other assailant, still not knowing where the help had come from.

"It's me, Barry Raeburn, Ian." He had time to gasp out, as they fought. Raeburn had his man spread-eagled on the grass below him, and eased the hands on the throat while there was life in the body. He was aware of the near regret with which he recognised the relaxation of surrender, marking the fact that his victim had given up and was hoping for life.

"Aye, ye did well, the two of ye," said the voice of Reid as if from the sky. He seemed to tower immensely above them, as he bent with the stun gun in his hand. "Your fellow first, Mr. Raeburn. There now," and the bellow from the muzzle lifted Raeburn's man. In a moment Rankine was rising also, leaving his opponent in the first stages of the long sleep.

"To tell ye the truth," Reid was saying, "I saw Mr. Rankine here doing fine, and I didn't want tae spoil his ploy, so I gave him a wee while with the twa gentry. Anyway, we're all here and nane the worse."

"A bit breathless, that's all," Raeburn said. "I suppose we'll have to get these fellows back to the bunker, for stacking."

"No need at all, sir," said Reid. "There's nae point in giving oorsels mair work. They'll be quite comfortable here until the morning, and a wee while beyond that. Let them lie."

"Good idea," Raeburn said. "I wasn't keen to face that slope again."

"What now?" was Rankine's query.

Reid coughed deferentially. "If I might suggest it, gentlemen, Mr. Rankine might go with me for a turn around the tower, for it's there they might be tempted to forgather. My opinion is that we are near the end of this carry-on. Mr. Raeburn is fine on his own—him being like the laird o' the place. We'll see ye at the bunker, sir. Gie's a bit o' a shout if ye are in trouble."

Once more Raeburn went into the thicker trees and almost at once was aware of a figure skulking in a crouch. He followed it quietly, unable to tell if it was a Markland man or an enemy. Soon he realised it was not one of his own, but there was something in the posture that did not fit with one of Milligan's people.

The man froze suddenly, detected. And turning, made a rush for Raeburn, who put out the right hip and threw him over the buttock, so that they both landed grappling. This was a different class of assailant. There was something of a steely fitness, a lean bulging of muscle and hardness and training altogether apart from Milligan's men. They rolled, fighting for the topmost position, and the man prevailed, so that Raeburn found himself on his back, gripping the figure on top by the clothing on his shoulder blades, and realising that the right hand of the other was freeing itself to get at some weapon.

They lay like this, both with spread legs. There was a sudden thud as a third figure landed with a leap on the back of Raeburn's foe, driving half the breath from the fighting pair. Raeburn was aware of a pair of lean knees pressing his clutching fists, and ready hands forcing upwards in helplessness the grip that had already freed a knife.

The newcomer spoke. "Let it go or I'll break your arm."

Unbelievable! It was a woman's voice, and it had more menace than a hundred Milligans. It was Pamela Wilson.

Again she said, "I'm going to break it! Now!"

"Okay," said the man on top, and Raeburn felt him relax.

Raeburn said, "Who are you? Identify yourself."

There was a pause. Then the voice said, "Olsen, Rick. Captain, U.S. Marine Corps."

16

The man who had spoken with the Texas accent relaxed still further. But Raeburn felt his own grip tighten, and so did the pinioning knees. The three froze even harder into a muscular knot, straining for understanding—for belief.

It was Raeburn who responded first. "Say that again. Identify yourself! Who are you?"

The man said levelly, "Olsen, Rick. Captain, U.S. Marine Corps. My turn now: Who are you?"

"Raeburn, Barry. Headmaster of Markland School."

Their captive gave a choked gurgle of laughter; then said, "Glad to know you. I have letters for you. Maybe I could get my arm back from the lady wrestler."

The heap eased and unknotted, and suddenly they were all on their feet. By some quick instinct of relief their arms were round each other again, and they yielded to laughter.

Raeburn felt it time at last to break off, saying, "Quiet, everybody!"

The very oddity of their circumstance, and even their physical posture, gave them up again to mirth, this time to a suppressed giggle. They held it for some seconds, and when they let it die away, Raeburn and Pamela Wilson waited for Captain Olsen to speak.

He said, "I don't know how much time we have, fellows, but I better tell you. I have a small squad here—half a dozen altogether—and we're here to collect young Mackay. I believe you were expecting us?"

"Yes," said Raeburn. "Though we had no idea when and

where, and as a rule we are not out and about and ready for visitors in the middle of the night. You are the second lot here on the same mission. You said you have letters?"

"All you'll need. Can we go to the bunker and let you read them in comfort?"

"The bunker! What do you know about that?"

"Part of the job. It's a joint project of the western defence system. I know all about it, but of course I've never been there. Looking forward to seeing it."

The captain took a small silver instrument on a lanyard. "I'll call in my squad," he said. "You won't hear anything, but they will home in on me." He seemed to blow, but all they heard was breath. "Let's go," he said.

As they walked through the sparsely lit growth, other figures joined them. By the time they were at the door, the marine group numbered five and their captain. They stood, alert and silent.

Raeburn gave the double knock and ushered them in. The marines gathered, and there was a brief explanation to the Markland people. All of them listened as the headmaster rushed through the details of the Milligan team, and the newcomers inspected the sprawled heap of those who had been captured.

"I'd say you've done well, Mr. Raeburn. Not much left for us to do. How many, would you say?"

"I imagine six or seven at the most. The leader, Milligan, is armed."

"Okay. Best thing to do now is call in your own people. Let us do the rest. Here are your letters. Can I see the Mackay boy?"

Raeburn signalled to Pamela Wilson, and she took the microphone that the boy had ready for her.

"Attention, Markland men! This is important. Come at once to the door—to the door. Now!"

Captain Olsen was already talking to Michael Mackay. "Not long before we're on our way. When I saw you got the flag up, I knew we were on a winner. Not many people would've broken that signal." They exchanged speech charged with jargon. A marine sergeant had already gathered the rest of the squad round the spread maps. Shortly after Olsen joined them, they listened in silence as they pointed and explained.

There were three letters for Raeburn. One was from Mackay's father, written from his office in Hong Kong, agreeing to the transfer of his son by the marines to the United States. The second was an identification of Olsen and his men, instructing them to make the journey and to receive cooperation from the headmaster and the proper authorities. The third was unmistakably from the proper authorities, signed by two British cabinet ministers, the Foreign Secretary and the Secretary of State for Defence, both of whom Raeburn knew. He had been at school with one of them.

Ian Rankine was one of the first to arrive back at the bunker. Raeburn made him read the letters and sign and date them as a witness. The others were drifting in and hearing the same explanation and greeting the marines. Hugh Beattie was one of the last, and he was dragging another victim, whom he threw down on the heap.

"He's been attended tae by wan o' the gamekeepers. Handy chaps, these. But who the hell," he grumbled, "is spilin' the fun? Surely we havenae surrendered or what."

He was easily reassured and moved heartily among the marines. "I've heard o' you chaps. Who hasnae?"

Raeburn said to Olsen, "All our people are inside now, Captain. What now?"

"We go out and get them. We'll do a drive line across the width of the grounds, and I reckon one sweep will do it—two at the most. I hope we don't need to shed blood, but these are hostile men who are armed, and we may have to shoot first. Say —can anyone explain what this Milligan looks like?"

Michael Mackay said, "I think I saw more of him than anybody else. Very tall—no headgear—walks with his shoulders like this—head shaped like—see, I'll try to draw him." He turned over one of the maps and traced outlines. "He has these big tufts of hair sticking out from the side of his head. None of the others has anything like it."

"That should do. Thanks, Mike. See you all soon. How long until daylight?"

"Two and a half hours." Raeburn saw them through the steel doors.

Macfarlane went with them, packing the stun gun, and saying, "I know them. I was with them at the Rhine."

"What a curtain line!" Raeburn joined the others. There were more stories to tell, and especially the one about Miss Wilson's leap upon the prostrate marine captain. "Amazing," said Dr. Allen. He went to sit beside her, saying, "Tell me your version."

Raeburn sat among the gadgetry with young Mackay, taping one by one the experience of each of the Markland people. Fletcher offered a comic lament. "I never did a single heroic thing," he said, "except half murder the enemy wi' my music. I never even did a heid-banger wi' the frying pan, like the cook here."

The marines, strung across the woodland part and bushes of the grounds, swept their line forward slowly, well-drilled. Twice a man rose before them and turned to run, to be brought down with a breathless bump. Macfarlane was up with the capture at once, to administer the double roe deer, and each time he said, "Just let him lie here. He'll be easy enough picked up later."

At the center of the line, Olsen was moving firmly, his gun out and ready. Each man had fitted a silencer, but no shot had yet been fired. Ahead of him there rose suddenly a great tall figure, his shoulders moving as Mackay had described. His head was haloed by the three-quarter moon behind him, which lit like silver the tufts that stood out at each side. The man had a weapon in his hand.

"I see you there," he said.

Olsen's bullet took him exactly in the middle of the forehead, between the two tufts of hair. Milligan went backwards, flat and rigid. He could not have even heard the cough of Olsen's weapon.

Immediately three other figures stood up on the same spot, arms high, and all were calling, "Don't shoot!"

Olsen called with his silver whistle, and his men materialised from the wings. "Lights!" called the captain, and a bright beam swept round the group and onto the dead man and his surrendering companions.

"We're all here, Captain," the sergeant announced.

"Me too," Macfarlane said from the rear. He stepped to the fallen man, looked briefly, and turned away with, "That's one of my bullets saved." He stood over behind the prisoners, saying to Olsen, "These—eh, Captain?"

Olsen nodded. "Sure."

As Macfarlane came forward with his stun gun, two of the men started to whimper, in the certainty of execution. "You're not dead yet," said the gamekeeper patiently. In succession each pair of arms dropped, and the bodies went limp a second or two after they took the charge. "That'll be the lot, you may be sure." The hillman tucked his weapon out of sight.

"Okay, fellows—back to base." Olsen led the way to the Giant's Grave.

In the bunker the Markland people gathered to hear the brief story. Raeburn, who had been compiling a log of events after the taping, made the entries and pushed the book over to Olsen. "I'd be glad if you entered the bare facts as they affect us. We shall probably have to make some accounting sometime. Exercise your own military censorship at your discretion."

He turned to Ridley, who was still listening, agog.

"You, chef! How about breakfast for our guests? Some sort of meal anyway."

Ridley stepped forward importantly and took the floor. "What is it to be, gentlemen—and Miss Wilson? Anything you fancy. Lots of coffee ready—and corned beef hash, rashers and eggs, hash browns, waffles and maple syrup—all ready in a few minutes. I'll take your orders now."

"I don't believe it," moaned one of the marines.

"I served for three years on the cruise liners," said Ridley to Raeburn. "I know what they like."

Calder and Pamela Wilson set the table. It was a memorable feast, and unexpected, with occasional cries of delight directed at the red-faced Ridley, sweating with achievement, as he served endless courses. They drank the health of the Queen and the President, and at the end of it all Fletcher took his violin and marched round the table again and again, playing a long reveille, with all the old gallant march tunes.

They were cheering him as he finished, until a telephone rang loudly from the balcony. Michael darted up the ramp for it, with Raeburn after him. The boy answered, and in a moment said, "One second, ma'am. He's here."

He handed over the instrument with, "It's the Duchess for you, sir."

"Barry, is everybody all right?"

"Yes, by the grace of God. What about you?"

"All unscathed, and the girls are happily asleep. I've been calling every half hour, and the telephones have only now been connected. Tell me what happened."

"Too long a story. Things to do. Later."

"Understood. I'll bring the girls to the school tomorrow in time for the assembly."

"I'll get Pamela Wilson to fill you in. She's here."

"I might have guessed it."

"Edith, how on earth did you—"

"Another long story. We have the number of the bunker, and I thought it likely you would be there. Barry, you'd better get on with the job." She hung up.

Reid was at his elbow. "The telephone, Mr. Raeburn. Can I use it?"

"Sure. Not for long, please. There are some important calls to make."

"This is one of them, sir. To my cousin, the deputy chief constable."

"Good! I want to speak to him. What makes you think he will be at headquarters?"

"He'll no'. He'll be in his bed at hame, no' like the rest o' us here. I'll dig him oot."

He did no more than identify himself to his kinsman, then said, "Mr. Raeburn is here, Davie, and he wad like a wee word wi' ye." He handed over the phone.

Raeburn spent a few moments in apology for the intrusion, to be interrupted by the other with, "Fair enough, Mr. Raeburn. I'm used to late calls. I know fine you wouldn't be on unless there was something. What's your story?"

It did not take many minutes in the telling, with a very few brisk questions from the policeman. At the end Reid said, "Well, you've had a busy time. Sorry I missed it. It looks like the sort of setup we dealt with the other day. I'll have to refer it to that other authority—I'll do it from here. Then I'll have to call my chief, but I'll be back to you very soon. I have the bunker number. Been in it, in fact. 'Bye, now."

Captain Olsen had the marines grouped around him, with Michael Mackay in their midst. The officer came forward. "We'll need to be on our way, headmaster. I want to be airborne by first light."

Raeburn asked, "Have you got transport?"

"We have. A big truck parked near the gates on the outside."

"Where are you heading? Prestwick?"

Olsen was cool and bland, used to fending off the amateur-style question. He said, "Best you don't ask, headmaster." He held out a hand. "Glad to know you, Mr. Raeburn. I'll be putting in a report, but you won't likely be asked any questions. We had a good wee skirmish"—he gave it a Texan's version of a Scotch accent—"and you'll know how to get rid of the bodies.

I'll look you up one day in the future—socially. So long. Mike—
we're on our way."

He shook their hands at the door. Michael Mackay, briefly at
his elbow, said, "They are picking up my stuff at the tower. I'll
write you a long letter, Mr. Raeburn. Thanks for everything,
sir." He offered a handshake and was gone.

Raeburn let the door stand open to watch them in the darkness. *Is that all?* he thought to himself, conscious of the passing of
his own years. *Is there nothing more I could have done? What will they
do for him? To him?*

He turned from the useless reverie to find Macfarlane crush-
ing past him, saying, "Reid is waiting to hear from the cousin.
I'm off to put the vehicles back in order for the road." He swung
the bag of distributors and was off, saying, "Nothing much to do
except tidy up now. *Another one way,* thought Raeburn, *twenty
years older than me, and perhaps twice as efficient.*

Already Ridley was out of the kitchen, beaming with accomplishment, the chef's hat and apron laid aside. "All shipshape
and in order there," he announced. "Not a spoon out of place.
We made a good team, eh, Mr. Raeburn?"

"Hang on. Not finished yet." As Raeburn spoke, the phone
pealed, and he reached out to take it.

"That you, Mr. Raeburn? It's David Reid. I've cleared up
most of the problem, I think. Instructions from that other authority, as follows: No information of any kind to be given to the
public. The captured to be loaded into one of the stolen vehicles
and driven to a certain lay-by this side of Dumfries that is well-
known to my cousin. An escort will be waiting there to take over
the van, and that will probably be the last you will hear of them.
Over the next few days my men will pick up the other vehicles
from the school grounds. They are probably mostly stolen, and
we shall have records of ownership. There will be no action
required from you. We'll recover your car too. Is that all clear?
I'd be glad if you didn't require any more information. Now,
may I speak to the other Reid?"

Ian Rankine came through the door to Raeburn's side. "Barry, we don't have to carry the sleeping beauties all the way. I have brought out a school garbage truck. It's at the foot of the Giant's Grave hill now. Not far."

The inert bodies still lay huddled, like sleeping pups. After the strenuous work of the night, it seemed a relief to hump them down the short hill and into the truck in a heap. Hugh Beattie took his normal two, and soon they were loaded. At the van Macfarlane had the engine running, and he and Reid had pushed the other men aboard. Milligan was already on the van floor, a tarpaulin around him.

"Ready to go, Mr. Raeburn," said Macfarlane. "I'll follow Reid in the estate wagon and take him back. Likely we'll see you again soon, sir. Look after yourself, if we are not about."

He swung away, and then turned back to say softly, "Reid will call the Duke and tell him. He knows what to say. I mean, don't you bother, sir, to say anything, you know?"

The van and the estate car fled into the night, and the small remaining contingent watched them go. It seemed their group had come closer together, as if for comfort or companionable unity, bound in a comradship they would never quite lose. Dr. Allen had put his heavy coat over Pamela Wilson's shoulders.

"What now?" asked Ian Rankine.

"Now?" Raeburn repeated. "Now we get to bed and have a few hours' sleep. End-of-term day tomorrow—no, today. Busy time. No morning run, but bright and early for the assembly. No speeches now, but thank you, everybody. That's all, I think."

"Bloody good, too!" said Hugh Beattie. "I wouldnae mind a wee doss mysel'. There's a helly a lot o' plumbing to be done the morn. Come on, Murdo Fletcher, see me tae ma bed. We had a lot o' fun, though."

The low morning sun flooded through a window and into the shower where Barry Raeburn stood luxuriating. He was allowing the warm water to relax him, and he smiled to realise that he had been carolling to himself such snatches as "Wash all my sins away"—an old habit that he was not likely to give up. He lingered, feeling cleansed, above all of tiredness, and anyway knowing he would shortly have to endure the change to the ice-cold deluge, a brief agony, worth postponing, but which would condition him for the day ahead. Hardly two hours now, and they would all be gone.

He heard the tap at the door, telling him that Ridley had arrived with the breakfast tray. The usual ritual was for Ridley to put the tray down and depart silently. This morning he was in the mood to spin out the ceremony.

"Breakfast, Mr. Raeburn."

"Thank you. Just leave it on the table, please."

There was a pause. "None the worse, eh?"

"Not a bit. And you?"

"All the better, thank you, sir."

By the time he went through the front door, it was to find parents already arriving. He was able to greet some of them before they were escorted away on the informal tour of inspection. At some point the Duchess arrived, driving an estate wagon out of which the girls swarmed. She said, "I thought of coming to the assembly. May I?"

"Nobody more welcome, as I've said. Seats at the back for parents and friends—and patrons."

"Good. The adventure story will keep until later. We've nothing to report from Kintalla."

The assembly was almost a repeat of yesterday's, perhaps more impressive because it was the real thing, and the parents were there, many of whom had not been at any kind of religious service for years. Calder, the school captain, read through the Bible passage that Raeburn had selected, and at last it was over. They poured out to the cars and buses. Raeburn took up his stance halfway down the main drive and waved them all away. Some stopped to offer handshakes through open doors, and buses slowed to cheer him.

One of the last to come was Ian Rankine, driving alone. He drew to the side to say, "Barry, what are you doing for the holidays?"

"Nothing fixed, really. When they find my car, I might take to the road—I don't know where."

"Well, you know, Angela and I have this wee place in Elie. I'm going straight there now. There's always a bed for you there. Let us know. We owe you a lot. All the best."

Raeburn walked slowly to the main building. One car still waited there. Dr. Allen was driving, and his daughter Frances was in the rear seat. They waved good-bye.

The passenger door opened, and from it came Pamela Wilson, walking towards him. "Barry," she said, "just to say au revoir and all the best. Will you get any kind of holiday?"

"Well, if they get my car back, I'll probably take to the road. What about you? I see they're giving you a lift. What then?"

She paused, not disconcerted. "In fact, I'm going home with the Allens. The doctor wants me to be hostess for the dance he is arranging for Frances. I thought it would be best if I saw the whole arrangement through."

Unexpectedly, she had coloured a little and had lost a little of her poise. He looked her over, appraising the smart suit she wore.

"Very becoming," he said suddenly. And at once they both knew he was not talking of her outfit but of the blush that spread remorselessly over her fine features.

Without a word more, she turned and walked to the car. "Be happy," he said after her. She half raised a gloved hand in salute and did not look back.

17

They were all gone, and he was alone. And in a strange way, like the bereaved, he felt liberated. He was accustomed to this sense of isolation, since the great adventure of partnership had never come his way. He had not resisted it or fiercely sought it, believing that if it was meant for him, it would emerge, like the blossoms on the trees in spring.

So he walked the empty grounds and counted his blessings. It was his lairdship, and the many boys and the few girls were his family, and more desirable than many families he had known. Not many had almost the sole responsibility for such a clan, and there were some who in their turn would bring back to the school some renown. At this moment young Mackay would be landing in some not too alien spot and would be greeted as one already carrying splendour with him, with much more to come. There were others. For a moment he thought fondly of the future opening, one might hope, to Pamela Wilson, whose sudden vision of fulfillment had seemed to come from nowhere. For himself, he saw the future as clear—and solitary. Within that vision for himself, he sought contentment.

He saddened briefly at the thought that there had not been time to bid some sort of farewell to the Duchess. She must have noticed his preoccupations with parents and pupils, and had herself slipped away to take up the tasks that awaited her. It was a pity, in some sense, because she was solitary, like himself.

There was nothing more to do. If the car was found, he would load and go aimlessly and not unhappily into the far north. His tasks here were finished. Later in the day would come the caretaking and cleaning squads, and everything could be left to them.

He went back to his quarters in the main school building, where he would rest and perhaps read. Opening the door, he saw that she was there.

She did not look up from her task. She was packing his old travelling suitcase, laid out neatly on the bed. At its side was a pile of discarded and worn shirts, and two suits. He saw that she had changed into light tweeds, with her hair no longer piled up and orderly, but loose and flowing in a red cascade.

As he watched, she said, "I thought this suit rather than that one. Most of this stuff can be left. We can get other things when we arrive. I've put aside your passport and traveller's cheques."

"What is this, Edith?" he said at last.

"We're going away. Three weeks is about right. Long overdue. We are both lonely. Where would you fancy? I have empty houses everywhere—Italy, Kenya, California, Morocco. . . . But we have time to decide."

"Edith, I can't manage—"

"The money? No problem. He must have told you. He tells everybody who matters. What he doesn't know is that my dear old Aunt Molly—you know, Lady Molly Miles—gave me most of her jewelry. I had a dealer come to Kintalla the other day and flogged him some for over seven thousand pounds. That should be enough. We'll sleep tonight at Allenhope."

Allenhope was the greatest estate in the north of England, three times the size of Kintalla, and the Duke derived from it one of his noblest titles.

They loaded his case into the Iglietti, which was parked at the back door, and she boomed the engine to life. "We're away," she said.

He sat beside her as they travelled east and then south. There was not much speaking. More and more he simply relaxed to her nearness. She was the liberator, the protector, and comforter: the one who knew. After a time his head leaned upon her shoulder, and he slept.

ABOUT THE AUTHOR

Alastair Dunnett trained and qualified as a banker but he later became editor of the two most important daily newspapers in Scotland, *The Daily Record* and *The Scotsman*. At the start of the North Sea oil boom he became Chairman of a Scottish-based offshore oil company. He has written stage plays, has had books published in Great Britain and the United States, and is well known as a commentator on radio and television. He is married to Dorothy Dunnett, a historical novelist, and they live in Edinburgh, Scotland. They have two sons.